Apart from enjoying an enviable reputation as one of the best writers on the science fiction scene, Harry Harrison is a man of wide interests and accomplishments.

A first class short story writer, an experienced editor and anthologist (compiler, with Brian Aldiss, of Sphere's *Year's Best SF* series), a translator (from Danish and Italian), a trained cartoonist, he has also been a commercial illustrator, hydraulic press operator, truck driver and is, of course, a first rate novelist.

Harrison's style leaps from the humour of his *Stainless Steel Rat* novels to purist sf to the splendid combination of fantasy and science fiction found in *Captive Universe*.

D1494434

Also by Harry Harrison in Sphere Books

THE STAINLESS STEEL RAT
THE STAINLESS STEEL RAT SAVES THE WORLD
THE STAINLESS STEEL RAT WANTS YOU
DEATHWORLD 1, 2 and 3
TWO TALES AND EIGHT TOMORROWS
NOVA 2, 3 and 4
CAPTIVE UNIVERSE
PLAGUE FROM SPACE

The Stainless Steel Rat's Revenge

HARRY HARRISON

SPHERE BOOKS LIMITED
30-32 Gray's Inn Road, London WC1X 8JL

First published in Great Britain by Faber and Faber Ltd 1971
Copyright © Harry Harrison 1970
Published by Sphere Books Ltd 1974
Reprinted 1976, 1977, 1978 (twice), 1979, 1980, 1981

TRADE
MARK

Set in Intertype Times

Printed and bound in Great Britain by
©ollins, Glasgow

CHAPTER ONE

I STOOD IN LINE, as patient as the other taxpayers, my filled out forms and my cash gripped hotly in my hand. Cash, money, the old fashioned folding stuff. A local custom that I intended to make expensive to the local customers. I was scratching under the artificial beard, which itched abominably, when the man before me stepped out of the way and I was at the window. My finger stuck in the glue and I had a job freeing it without pulling off the beard as well.

'Come, come, pass it over,' the aging, hatchet-faced, bitter and shrewish female official said, hand extended impatiently.

'On the contrary,' I said, letting the papers and banknotes fall away to disclose the immense .75 recoilless pistol that I held. '*You* pass it over. All of that tax money you have extracted from the sheeplike suckers who populate this backward planet.'

I smiled to show that I meant it and she choked off a scream and began scrabbling in the cash drawer. It was a broad smile that showed all of my teeth, which I had stained bright red, which should have helped her decide on the proper course of action. As the money was pushed towards me I stuffed it into my long topcoat that was completely lined with deep pockets.

'What are you doing?' the man behind me gasped, eyes bulging like great white grapes.

'Taking money,' I said and flipped a bundle at him. 'Why don't you have some yourself.' He caught it by reflex,

5

goggled at it, and all the alarms went off at once and I heard the doors crashing shut. The cashier had managed to trigger an alarm.

'Good for you,' I said, 'but don't let a minor thing like that prevent you from keeping the cash coming.'

She gasped and started to slip from sight, but a wave of the gun and another flash of my carmine dentures restored a semblance of life, and the flow of bills continued. People started to rush about and gun waving guards began to appear looking round enthusiastically for someone to shoot, so I triggered the radio relay in my pocket. There was a series of charming explosions all about the bank, from every wastebasket where I had planted a gas bomb, followed by the even more charming screams of the customers. I stopped stowing money long enough to slip on the gas-tight goggles and settle them into place. And to clamp my mouth shut so I was forced to breathe through the filter plugs in my nostrils.

It was fascinating to watch. Blackout gas is invisible and has no odor but it does contain a chemical that acts almost instantly, bringing about a complete but temporary paralysis of the optic nerve. Within fifteen seconds everyone in the bank was blind.

With the exception of James Bolivar diGriz, myself, man of many talents. Humming a happy tune through closed lips I stowed away the remaining money. My benefactress had finally slid from sight and was screaming incontinently somewhere behind the counter. So were a lot of other people. There was plenty of groping about and falling over things as I made my way through this little blacked out corner of bedlam. An eerie sensation indeed, the one-eyed man in the country of the blind and all that. A crowd had already gathered outside, pressing in fascinated awe against the windows and glass doors, to watch the drama unfolding inside. I waved and smiled and a shudder passed through the nearest as they pushed back in panic from the door. I shot the lock out, angling the gun so the bullets shrieked away over their heads, and kicked the doors open. Before exiting myself I threw a screamer out onto the sidewalk and quickly pushed the stoppers into my ears.

The screamer sounded and everyone began to leave quickly. You *have* to leave quickly when you hear one of these things. They send out a mixed brew of devilish sounds at the decibel level of a major earthquake. Some are audible, sounds like a magnified fingernail on a blackboard, while others are supersonic and produce sensations of panic and imminent death. Harmless and highly effective. The street was otherwise empty when I walked out to the car that was just pulling up to the curb. My head was throbbing with the supersonics that got past the plugs and I was more than happy to slip through the open door and relax while Angelina gunned the machine down the street.

'Everything go all right?' she asked, keeping her eyes on the road as she whipped around a corner on the outside wheels. Sirens began to sound in the distance.

'A piece of cake. Smooth as castor oil . . .'

'Your similes leave a lot to be desired.'

'Sorry. A touch of indigestion this morning. But my coat is lined with more money than we could possibly need.'

'How nice!' she laughed, and she meant it. That irresistible grin, the crinkled nose. I longed to nibble it, or at least kiss her, but settled for a comradely pat on the shoulder since she needed all her concentration for driving. I popped a stick of gum in my mouth that would remove the red tooth dye and began to peel off my disguise.

As I changed so did the car. Angelina turned into a side street, slowed and then found an even quieter street to drive along. There was no one in sight. She pressed the button.

My, but technology can do some interesting things. The license plate flipped over to reveal a different number, but that was too simple a trick to even discuss. Angelina flicked on the windscreen wipers as a fine spray of catalytic fluid sprang out of jets on the front of the car. Wherever it touched the blue paint turned a bright red. Except for the top of the car which became transparent so that in a few moments we were sitting in a bubble-top surveying the world around. A good deal of what appeared to be chrome plated metal dissolved and washed away altering the appearance and even the make of the car. As soon as this process was complete Angelina sedately turned a corner and started back in the direction from whence we had come. Her orange wig was locked away with my disguise and I held the wheel while she put on an immense pair of goggly sunglasses.

'Where to next?' she asked as a huddle of shrieking police cars tore by in the opposite direction.

'I was thinking of the shore. Wind, sun, sand, that sort of thing. Healthy and bracing.'

'A little too bracing if you don't mind my saying so.' She patted the rounded bulge of her midriff with a more than satisfied smile. 'It's six months now, going on seven, so I'm not feeling that athletic. Which reminds me . . .' She flashed me a quick scowl, then turned her attention back to the road. 'You promised to make an honest woman out of me so that we could call this a honeymoon.'

'My love,' I said, and clasped her hand in all sincerity. 'At the first possible moment. I don't want to make an honest woman out of you – that would be physically impossible since you are basically as larcenous minded as I am – but I will certainly marry you and slip an expensive—'

'Stolen!'

'—ring on this delicate little finger. I do promise. But the second we try to register a marriage we'll be fed into the computer and the game will be up. Our little holiday at an end.'

8

'And you'll be hooked for life. I think I better grab you now before I get too round to run and catch you. We'll go to your beach resort and enjoy one last day of mad freedom. And tomorrow, right after breakfast, we are getting married. Do you promise?'

'There is just one question . . .'

'Promise, Slippery Jim, I know you!'

'You have my word except . . .'

She braked the car to a skidding stop and I found myself looking down the barrel of my own .75 recoilless. It looked very big. Her knuckle was white on the trigger.

'Promise you quick-witted slippery tricky crooked lying con man or I'll blow your brains out.'

'My darling, you *do* love me!'

'Of course I do. But if I can't have you all to myself I'll have you dead. Speak!'

'We get married in the morning.'

'Some men are *so* hard to convince,' she whispered, slipping the gun into my pocket and herself into my arms. Then she kissed me with such delicious intensity that I almost looked forward to the morrow.

CHAPTER TWO

'WHERE ARE YOU GOING, SLIPPERY JIM?' Angelina asked, leaning out of the window of our room above. I stopped with my hand on the gate.

'Just down for a quick swim, my love,' I shouted back and swung the gate open. A .75 roared and the ruins of the gate were blown out of my hand.

'Open your robe,' she said, not unkindly, and blew the smoke from the gun barrel at the same time.

I shrugged with resignation and opened the beach robe. My feet were bare. But of course I was fully dressed, with my pants' leg rolled up and my shoes stuffed into my jacket pockets. She nodded understandingly.

'You can come back upstairs. You're going nowhere.'

'Of course I'm not.' Hot indignation. 'I'm not that sort of chap. I was just afraid you might misunderstand. I just wanted to nip into the shops and . . .'

'Upstairs.'

I went. Hell hath no fury etc. was invented to describe my Angelina. The Special Corps medics had stripped her of her homicidal tendencies, unknotted the tangled skeins of her subconscious and equipped her for a more happy existence than circumstance had previously provided. But when it came to the crunch she was still the old Angelina. I sighed and mounted the stairs with leaden feet.

And I felt even more of an unthinking fiend when I saw that she was crying. 'Jim, you don't love me!' A classic gambit since the first woman in the garden, but still unanswerable.

'I do,' I protested, and I meant it. 'But, it's just . . . reflex. Or something like that. I love you, but marriage is, well, like going to prison. And in all my crooked years I have never been sent up.'

'It is liberation, not captivity,' she said and did things with her makeup that removed the ravages of the tears. I noticed for the first time that she had white lipstick on to match her white dress and a little lacy kind of thing in her hair.

'This is just like going swimming in cold water,' she said, standing and patting my cheek. 'Get it over with quickly so you won't feel it. Now roll down your pants and put those shoes on.'

I did, but when I straightened up to answer this last fatuous argument I saw that the door had opened and that a Marriage Master and his two witnesses were standing in the next room. She took my arm, gently, I'll say that for her, and at the same time the recorded strains of the mighty organ filled the air. She tugged at my elbow, I resisted for a moment, then lurched forward as a gray mist seemed to fall over my eyes.

When the darkness lifted the organ was bleating its dying notes, the door was closing behind the departing backs and Angelina stopped admiring her ring-decorated finger long enough to raise her lips to mine. I had barely enough strength of will left to kiss her first before I groaned.

There were a number of bottles on the sideboard and my twitching fingers stumbled through them to unerringly find a knobby flask of Syrian Panther Sweat, a potent beverage with such hideous aftereffects that its sale is forbidden on most civilized worlds. A large tumbler of this was most efficacious, I could feel it doing me harm, and I poured a second one. While I was doing this and immersed in my numbed thoughts a period of time must have passed because Angelina – *my* Angelina (suppressed groan) – now stood

11

before me dressed in slacks and sweater with our bags packed and waiting at her side. The glass was plucked from my fingers.

'Enough private whoopee,' she said, not unkindly. 'We'll celebrate tonight but right now we have to move. The marriage record will be filed at any moment and when our names hit the computer it's going to light up like a knocking shop on payday. By now the police will have tied us in to most of the crimes of the past two months and will come slavering and baying after us.'

'Silence,' I ordered, swaying to my feet. 'The image is a familiar one. Get the car and we will leave.'

I offered to help with the bags but by the time I communicated this information she was halfway down the stairs with them. With this encouragement I navigated the hazard and reached the door. The car was outside humming with unleashed power, the side door open and Angelina at the wheel tapping her foot with equally unleashed impatience. As I stumbled into it the first tentacles of reality penetrated my numbed cortex. This car, like all other ground cars on Kamata, was steam powered and the steam was generated by the combustion of a specie of peat bricks fed to the furnace by an ingenious and unnecessarily complicated device. It took at least half an hour to raise steam to get moving. Angelina must have fired up before the wedding and planned every other step as well. My solitary contribution to all this was a private drink which had been very little aid at all. I shuddered at what this meant, yet was still driven to the only possible conclusion.

'Do you have a drive-right pill?' I asked, hoarsely.

It was in the palm of her hand even as I spoke. Small, round, pink, with a black skull and crossbones on it. A sobering invention of some mad chemist that worked like a metabolic vacuum cleaner. Short minutes after hitting the hydrochloric acid pool of my stomach the ingredients

12

would be doing a blitzkrieg attack through my bloodstream. Not only does it remove all of the alcohol but strips away all of the side products associated with drinking as well, so that the pitiful subject is instantly cold sober and painfully aware of it.

'I can't take it without water,' I mumbled, blinking at the plastic cup in her other hand. There was no turning back. With a last happy shudder I flipped the deadly thing into the back of my throat and drained the cup.

They say it doesn't take long, but that is an objective time. Subjective was hours. It is a most unusual experience and difficult to describe. Imagine if you will what it feels like to take the nozzle of a cold water hose in your mouth and then to have the water turned on. And then, an instant later, to have the water gushing in great streams from every orifice of your body, including the pores, until you are flushed completely clean.

'Wow,' I said weakly, sitting up and dabbing at my forehead with my handkerchief. The houses of a small village rushed by and were replaced by farmlands. Angelina drove with calm efficiency and the boiler chunked merrily as it ate another brick of peat.

'Feeling better, I hope?' She dived into a traffic circle and left it by a different road with only a quick glimpse at the map. 'The alarm is out for us, army, navy, everything. I've been listening to their command radio.'

'Are we going to get away?'

'I doubt it – not unless you come up with some bright idea very quickly. They have a solid ring with aerial cover around the area and are tightening it.'

I was still recovering from the heroic treatment of the drive-right pill and had not collected all my wits. There was a direct connection from my muddled thoughts to my vocal cords that had no intervening censor of intelligence.

'A great start to marriage. If this is what it is like no wonder I have been avoiding it all these years.'

The car swung off the road and shuddered to a stop in the deep grass under a row of blue-leaved trees. Angelina was out, had slammed the door and was reaching for her bag before I had time to react. I tried to tell her.

'I'm a fool . . .'

'Then I'm a fool too for marrying you.' She was dry eyed and cold of voice with all of her emotions strictly under control. 'I tricked you and trapped you into marriage because it was what I thought you really wanted. I was wrong, so it's going to end right now before it really gets started. I'm sorry, Jim. You made an entirely new life for me and I thought I could make one for you. It has been fun knowing you. Thank you and good-bye.'

By the time she had finished, my thoughts had congealed into something roughly resembling their normal shape and I was weak but ready. I was out of the car before she had finished talking and standing in front of her, blocking her way, holding her most gently by the arms.

'Angelina, I will tell you this but once and probably never again the rest of my life. So listen well and remember. At one time I was the best crook in the galaxy, before I was conned into the Special Corps to help catch other crooks. And I caught you. Not only were you a crook but a mastermind criminal as well and a cheerfully sadistic murderess.' I felt her body shiver in my hands and held her tighter. 'It has to be said, because that is what you were. You aren't any more. You had reasons to be that way and the reasons have been removed and some unhappy quirks in your otherwise pristine cortex have been straightened out. And now I love you. But I want you to remember that I loved you even then during your unreconstructed days, which is saying a lot. So if I buck at the harness now, or

14

am difficult to deal with in the mornings, just remember that and make allowances. Is it a deal?'

It apparently was. She dropped the bag – on my toe, but I dared not flinch – and wrapped her arms around me and was kissing me and knocked me over into the deep grass and I had a jolly time kissing her right back. The newlywed effect I suppose you would call it, great fun . . .

We froze, rigid, as a pair of flywheel cycles moaned and skidded to a stop by our car. Only the police used these since they move a good deal faster than the peat-powered steamers. They are tricycle affairs with a great heavy flywheel encased between the rear wheels. They plugged them in at night so their motor-generators could run the flywheel up to top speed. During the day the flywheel generated electricity to drive the motors in each wheel. Very efficient and smog-free. Very dangerous.

'This is the car, Podder!' one of the police shouted out over the constant moan of the flywheels.

'I'll call it in. They can't have gone far. We sure have them trapped now!'

Nothing infuriates me like the bland assurances of petty officials. Oh yes, really trapped now. I growled deep in my throat as the other uniformed incompetent poked his nose around the car and gaped at our cozy cuddle in the grass. He was still gaping when I lunged an arm up and around his neck with a tight squeeze on his throat and pulled him down to join us. It was fun to watch his tongue come out and his eyes pop and his head turn red but Angelina spoiled it. She whipped off his helmet and rapped him smartly – and accurately – on the temple with the heel of her shoe. He turned off and I let him drop.

'And you talk about *me*,' my bride whispered. 'You've got more than a touch of the old sadist in your own makeup.'

'I called it in. Everybody knows. We've sure got them

15

now . . .' the enthusiastic remaining officer said, but his voice rattled to a stop when he looked down the muzzle of his associate's riot gun. Angelina dug a sleep capsule out of her bag and snapped it under his nose.

'And now what, boss?' she asked, smiling happily at the two black-uniformed, brass-buttoned figures by the side of the road.

'I have been thinking,' I said, and rubbed my jaw and frowned with deep concentration to prove it. 'We have had over four months of worryless holiday, but all good things must end. We could extend our leave. But it would be hectic to say the least and people would get hurt and you – while that is a fine shape – it is not quite the shape for flight and pursuit and general nastiness. Shall we return to the service from which we fled?'

'I was hoping you would say that. Morning sickness and bank robbery just don't seem to mix. It will be fun to get back.'

'Particularly since they will be so glad to see us. Considering that they turned down our request for leave and we had to steal that mail ship.'

'Not to mention all the expense money we have stolen because we couldn't touch our bank accounts.'

'Right. Follow me and we'll do this with style.'

We stripped off their uniforms and gently laid the snoring peace officers in the rear of the car. One had pink polkadot underwear while the other's was utilitarian black – but trimmed with lace. Which might have been local custom of dress but gave me second thoughts about the police on Kamata and I was glad we were leaving. Uniformed, helmeted, and goggled we hummed merrily down the road on our flywheel cycles waving to all the tanks and trucks that roared by the other way. Before there were too many screams and shouts of discovery I braked in the center of the road and signaled an armored car to a stop. Angelina swung her cycle behind them so that they would not find the sight of a pregnant officer too distracting.

'Got them cornered!' I shouted. 'But they have a radio so keep this off the net. Follow me.'

'Lead on!' the driver shouted, his mate nodding agreement while thoughts of rewards, fame, medals danced dazzlingly before their eyes. I led them to a deserted track into the woods that ended at a small lake complete with ramshackle boathouse and dock.

I braked, waved them to a stop, touched my fingers to my lips and tiptoed back to their car. The driver lowered the side window and looked out expectantly.

'Breathe this,' I said and flipped a gas grenade through the opening.

There was a cloud of smoke followed by gasps followed by two more silent uniformed figures snoring in the grass.

'Going to take a quick peek at their underwear?' Angelina asked.

'No. I want to maintain some illusions, even if they are false.'

The cycles rolled merrily down the dock and off into the water where they steamed and shortcircuited and made a lot of bubbles. As soon as the armored car had aired out we boarded and drove away. Angelina found the driver's untouched lunch and cheerfully consumed it. I avoided most of the main roads and headed back to the city where the command post was located at the central police station. I wanted to go where the big action was.

We parked in the underground garage, deserted now, and took the elevator to the tower. The building was almost empty, except for the command center, and I found an unoccupied office nearby and left Angelina there. Innocently amusing herself with the sealed – but easily opened – confidential files. I lowered my goggles into place and staged a dusty, exhausted entrance to control. I was ignored. The man I wanted to see was pacing the floor sucking on a long dead pipe. I rushed up and saluted.

'Sir, are you Mr. Inskipp?'

'Yar,' he muttered, his attention still on the great wall chart that theoretically showed the condition of the chase.

'Someone to see you, sir.'

'What? What?' he said, still distracted. Harold Peters Inskipp, director and mastermind of the Special Corps, not quite with it this day. He followed me out easily enough and I closed the door and slipped off the heavy goggles.

'We're ready to come home now,' I told him. 'If you can find a quiet way of getting us off this planet without the locals getting their greedy hands on us.'

His jaw clenched with anger and fractured the mouthpiece of the pipe into innumerable fragments. I led him, spitting out pieces of plastic, to the room where Angelina was waiting.

CHAPTER THREE

'ARRGH!' INSKIPP SNARLED, and shook the sheaf of papers in his hand so that they rattled like dry skeletal bones.

'Very expressive,' I snarled, slipping a cigar from my pocket humidor and holding it to my ear. 'But with a very minimal content of information. Could you be more explicit?' I pinched the cigar's small end and there was not the slightest crackle. Perfection.

'Do you know how many millions your crime wave has cost? The economy of Kamata . . .'

'Will not suffer an iota. The government will reimburse the institutions that suffered the losses and will then in turn deduct the same amount from its annual payment to the Special Corps. Which has more money than it can possibly use in any case. And look at the benefits bestowed in return. Plenty of excitement for the populace, increased sales of newspapers, exercise for the sedentary law enforcement officers – and that is an interesting story in itself – as well as field maneuvers that were a pleasure for everyone involved. Far from being annoyed they should pay us a fee for making all these exciting things possible.' I lit the cigar and blew out a great cloud of fragrant smoke.

'Don't play wise with me, you aging con man. If I turned you and your bride over to the Kamata authorities you would still be in jail 600 years from now.'

'Little chance of that, Inskipp, aging con man yourself. You are short of good field agents as it is. You need us more than we need you. So consider this chewing out at an end and get on with the business. I have been chastised.'

I tore a button off the front of my jacket and threw it across the desk to him. 'Here, rip off my medals and reduce me to the ranks. I am guilty. Next case.'

With a final simulated growl of anger he filed the papers in the wastebasket and took out a large red folder that buzzed threateningly when he touched it. His thumb print defused the security device and the folder dropped open.

'I have a top secret gravely important assignment here.'

'What other kind do I ever get?'

'It is hideously dangerous as well.'

'You are secretly envious of my good looks and have a death wish for me. Come on, Inskipp. Stop sparring and let me know what the deal is. Angelina and I can handle it better than the rest of your senile and feeble agents.'

'This job of work is for you alone. Angelina is, well . . .' His face reddened and he examined the file closely.

'Whoopee!' I shouted. 'Inskipp the killer, daredevil, master of men, secret power in the galaxy today. And he can't say the word *pregnant*! How about *baby*? Wait, *sex*, that is a goodie. You blush to think about it. Go ahead, say *sex* three times fast, it will do you good—'

'Shut up, diGriz,' he growled. 'At least you finally married her which shows you have a single drop of honesty in your otherwise rotten carcass. She stays behind. You go out on this one-man job. Probably leaving her a widow.'

'She looks awful in black so you can't get rid of me that easily. Tell.'

'Look at this,' he said, taking a roll of film from the folder and slipping in into a slot in his desk. A screen dropped down from the ceiling and the room darkened. The film began.

The camera had been handheld, the color was off at times, and it was most unprofessional. But it was the best home movie I had ever seen because the material was so good. Authentic, no doubt about it.

Someone was waging war. It was a sunny day with white puffs of cloud against a blue sky. And black puffs of antiaircraft fire in among them. But the fire was not heavy and there was not enough of it to stop the troop carriers that came in low and fast for landing. This was an average sized spaceport, with the buildings in the far background and some cargo ships nearby. Other aircraft roared in low and bomb explosions reached skyward from what must have been the defense positions. The impossibility of what was happening finally came home to me.

'Those are *spaceships*!' I gurgled. 'And space *transports*. Is some numbskull government so stupid as to think that it can succeed in an interplanetary war? What happened after they lost – and how does it affect me?'

The film ended and the lights came up again. Inskipp steepled his fingers on the desk and leered over them.

'For your information, Mr. Know-it-all, this invasion succeeded – and so did the other ones before it. This film was taken by a smuggler, one of our regular informants, whose ship was just fast enough to get away during the battle.'

This was a stopper. I dragged deeply on the cigar and considered what little I knew about interplanetary warfare. There was little enough to know. Because it just doesn't work. Maybe a few times in the galaxy when local conditions are right, say a solar system with two inhabited planets. If one planet is backward and the other advanced industrially the primitive one might be invaded successfully. But not if they put up any kind of a real defense. The distance-time relationships just don't make this kind of warfare practical. When every soldier and weapon and ration has to be lifted from the gravity well of a planet and carried across space the energy expenditure is considerable, the transport demands incredible and the cost unbelievable. If, in addition, the invader has to land in the face of determined opposition the invasion is impossible. And this is inside a solar system where the planets are practically touching on a galactic scale. The thought of warfare between planets of differing star systems is even more impossible.

But, once again, it has been proven that nothing is basically impossible if people want to tackle it hard enough. And things like violence, warfare and bloodshed are still hideously attractive to the lurking violence potential of mankind, despite the centuries of peace and stagnation. I had a sudden and depressing thought.

'Are you telling me that a successful interplanetary invasion has been accomplished?' I asked.

'More than one.' That evil smirk was decorating his face as he spoke.

'And you and the League would like to see this practice stopped?'

'Right on the head, Jim my boy.'

'And I am the sucker who has been picked for the assignment?'

He reached out, took my cigar from my numb fingers and dropped it into the ashtray – then solemnly shook my hand. 'It's your job. Go out there and win.'

I slipped my hand from his treacherous embrace, wiped my fingers on my pantsleg and grabbed back my cigar.

'I'm sure that you will see that I have the best funeral the Corps can afford. Now, would you care to squeeze out a few details or would you prefer to blindfold me and shoot me out in a one-way cargo rocket?'

'Temper, my boy, temper. The situation seems to be quite clear. There has been little word about this in the news media because of a certain political confusion surrounding the invasions, plus a rigid censorship by the planets under consideration. As we have reconstructed it – and good men have died getting this information – the responsible world

22

is named Cliaand, the third planet in the Epsilon Indi system. There are two score planets orbiting this sun, but only three are inhabitable. And inhabited. Cliaand took over both the sister worlds some years ago, but we considered this no cause for alarm. What is alarming is the fact that they have expanded their scope. *Interstellar* conquest, heretofore considered an impossibility. They have invaded and conquered *five* other planets in nearby systems and seem poised for bigger and better things. We don't know how they are doing it, but they must be doing something right. We have had agents on the conquered worlds but have learned little of value. The decision has been made, a high level one I assure you – you would stand and salute if you heard some of the names of the people involved – that we must get a man to Cliaand to root out the problem at the core of the woodpile and cut the Gordian knot.'

'Other than being contained in a mixed and disgusting metaphor I think the idea is a suicidal one. Instead of this we could . . .'

'You are going. There is no possible way to wriggle out of this one, Slippery Jim.'

I tried. But nothing worked. I was given a copy of all the known details, a cortex-recording of the language and the masterkey to a fast pursuit ship to take me there. I returned gloomily to our quarters where Angelina, tired of doing her hair and her nails, was throwing a knife at a head-sized target on the far wall. She was very good. Even underhand, after a quick draw from her arm sheath, she could hit the black spot of either eye.

'Let me get a pic of Inskipp,' I said. 'It will make a more interesting target and one that you can get a degree of pleasure out of.'

'Is that evil old man sending my darling out on a job?'

'That dirty old goat is trying to get me killed. The

assignment is so top secret I can't tell a soul about it, particularly you, so here are all the papers, read them for yourself.'

While she did this I slipped the Cliaand language recording into the stamping machine. This recorded the material directly on my cortex without the boring and time-consuming intermediary of any learning process. The first session would take about half an hour with a dozen or more reinforcing sessions after that. I would end up speaking the language and having one hell of a headache from all the electronic fingering of my synapses. But there was a period of total unconsciousness while the machine operated and that was just what I felt like at the moment. I slipped the helmet down over my ears, settled on the couch and pressed the button.

There was a flicker of no-time and Angelina was carefully lifting off the helmet and handing me a pill at the same instant. I swallowed it and kept my eyes closed while the pain ebbed away. Soft lips kissed mine.

'They are trying to kill you, but you will not let them. You will laugh and win and someday you will have Inskipp's job.'

I opened one eye a crack and looked at her jubilant expression.

'Come home with my shield or on it? Go to glory or the grave? Are you worried about me?'

'All of the time. But that is a wife's job. I certainly cannot stand in the way of your career—'

'I didn't know I had one until you told me just now.'

'—and will do everything I can to help.'

'You can't come with me, for a very obvious and protruding reason.'

'I know that. But I will be with you in spirit all the time. How are you going to land on this world?'

'Board my nimble pursuit ship, come in straight and fast behind a radar screen, zing down into the atmosphere—'

'And get blasted into your component atoms. Here, read this report by the survivor of the last ship to try this approach.'

I read it. It was most depressing. I threw it back with the others.

'I heed the warning. This planet appears to be militarized to the hilt. I'll bet even the house pets wear uniforms. Bulling in like that is approaching these people on their own terms, competing in the area where they are best organized. What they are not organized against is a little bit of guile, some larceny, a smooth approach covering a devious attack. Insinuate, penetrate, operate and extirpate.'

'All at once I am beginning not to like it,' my love said, frowning. 'You will take care of yourself, Jim? I don't think worrying would be good for me right now.'

'If you wish to worry, worry about the fate of this poor planet with Slippery Jim unleashed against them. Their conquests are at an end, they are as good as finished.'

I kissed her resoundingly and walked out, head high and shoulders back.

Wishing that I was one tenth as sure of myself as I had acted. This was going to be a very rough one.

CHAPTER FOUR

MY PLANNING HAD BEEN DETAILED, the preparations complex, the operation gigantic. I had received more than one shrill cry of pain from Inskipp about the cost, all of which I dutifully ignored. It was my neck in the noose, not his, and I was hedging all the bets that I could to assure my corporeal survival. But even the most complicated plan is eventually completed, the last details sewed up, the final orders issued. And the sheep led to the slaughter.

Baaa. Here I was, naked to the world, sitting in the bar of the intersystem spacer *Kannettava*, a glass of strong drink before me and a dead cigar clutched in my fingers. Listening to the announcement that we would be landing on Cliaand within the hour. I was naked, figuratively speaking of course. It had taken an effort of will and strong discipline to force myself to leave every article of an illegal nature behind. I had never done this before in my entire life. No minibombs, gas capsules, gigli saws, fingertip drills, card holdouts, phone tappers. Nothing. Not even the lock pick that was always fixed to my toenail. Or . . .

I grated my teeth at the thought and looked about me. The other revelers were knocking back the taxfree booze in a determined manner and none was looking at me. Slipping my wallet from my pocket I touched the seam at the top. And felt a certain stiffness. Memory, how it cuts both ways, revealing and clouding. My own subconscious was fighting against me. Only my conscious mind was at all enthusiastic about landing on Cliaand without any illegal devices. I squeezed the wallet hard in the right way and the tiny but incredibly strong lockpick dropped into my fingers. A work of art. I admired it when I raised my glass. And said good-bye. On the way back to my cabin I dropped it into a waste disposal. It would go on with the ship while I landed on this singularly inhospitable world.

Every report and interview indicated that Cliaand had the most paranoic customs men in the known universe. Contraband simply could not be smuggled in. Therefore I was not trying. I was just what I appeared to be. A salesman, representative of Fazzoletto-Mouchoir Ltd., dealers in deadly weapons. The firm existed and I was their salesman and no amount of investigation could prove otherwise. Let them try.

They did. Landing on Cliaand was not unlike going into prison. I, and the handful of other debarkees, trundled down the gangway and into a gray room of ominous aspect. We huddled together, under the eyes of watchful and heavily armed guards, while our luggage was brought and dumped nearby. Nothing happened until the gangway had been withdrawn and the *Kannettava* had departed. Then, one by one, we were called out.

I was not first and I welcomed the opportunity to examine the local types. They were supremely indifferent to us, stamping about in knee-high boots, fingering their weapons and keeping their chins up high. Their uniforms were all the same color, a color which at first glance might be mistaken for a very unmilitary hue of carmine, a purplish red. Very quickly I realized that this was almost exactly the color of blood, half arterial blue, half venous pink. It was rather disgusting and hard to avoid looking at. And, in addition, gave no small hint about the nature of the wearer.

All of the guards were on the large side and ran to protruding jaws and little piggy eyes. Their helmets looked like fiber-steel, with sinister black visors and transparent faceplates that could be dropped down. Each carried a gaussrifle, a multipurpose and particularly deadly weapon. High capacity batteries stored a really impressive electrical charge in the stock. When the trigger was depressed a strong magnetic field was generated in the barrel which accelerated the missile with a muzzle velocity that equaled any explosive cartridge weapon. And the gaussrifle was superior in that it had a more rapid rate of fire, made no sound, and shot out any one of an assortment of deadly missiles, from poison needles to explosive charges. The Corps had reports about this weapon but we had never seen one. I made plans to rectify that situation as soon as possible.

'Pas Ratunkowy,' someone shouted and I stirred to life as I remembered this was my cover name. I waved hesitantly and one of the guards stomped and clacked over to me. I do believe that he had metal plates on his heels to increase the militaristic effect. I looked forward to getting a pair of these boots as well: I was beginning to like Cliaand.

'You Pas Ratunkowy?'

'I am he, sir, at your service,' I answered in his native tongue, being careful to keep a foreign accent.

'Get your luggage. Come with me.'

He spun about and I had the temerity to call after him.

'But, sir, bags are too heavy to carry all at once.'

This time he impaled me with a cold, withering look and fingered his gaussrifle suggestively. 'Cart,' he finally snarled and stabbed a finger at the far side of the prison yard. I humbly went after cart. This was a drably efficient motorized platform that rolled along on small wheels. I quickly loaded my bags onto it and looked for my guide. He stood by a now open door with his finger even closer to the trigger than before. The electric motor whined at top speed and I galloped after the thing towards the door.

The inspection began.

How easy that is to say. But it is one of those simple statements like 'I dropped the atom bomb and it went off.' This was the most detailed and thorough inspection I had ever experienced and I was exceedingly happy that I had found that lockpick first.

There were ten men waiting in the smooth-walled antiseptically white room. Six took my baggage while the other four took me. The first thing they did was strip me mother naked and drop me onto a fluoroscope. A magnifying one. Seconds later they were conferring over a blown-up print of the fillings in my teeth. There was a mutual decision that one of them was unduly large and had a rather unusual shape. A sinister looking array of dental gadgetry emerged and they had the filling out in an instant. While the tooth was being refilled with enamel – I'll say that much for them – the original filling was being zapped by a spectroscope. They seemed neither depressed nor elated when its metallic content proved to be that of an accepted dental alloy. The search went on.

While my tender pink person was being probed one of the inquisitors produced a file of papers. Most of these were psigrams sent out after my landing application had been received. They had consulted Fazzoletto-Mouchoir Ltd., my employers, and had all the details of my job. It is a good thing that this was legitimate. I responded correctly to all the questions, inserting random sounds only twice when the physical examination probed a tender spot. This appeared to go well; at least the file was closed and put aside.

While this was going on I had been catching glimpses of the fate of my bags. They suffered more than I did. Each of them had been opened and emptied, the contents spread out on the white tables, and the bag was then methodically taken to pieces. To little pieces. The seams were cut open, the fastening removed, the handles dissected. And the resulting rubbish put in plastic bags, labeled and saved. No doubt for a later and more detailed inspection. My clothing was given only a perfunctory examination then pushed aside. I soon found out why. I would not be seeing it again until I left the planet.

'You will be issued with good Cliaand clothing,' one of my inquisitors announced. 'It is a pleasure to wear.' I doubted that very much but kept my silence.

'Is this religious symbol?' another asked, holding the photograph in his fingertips at arm's length.

'It is a picture of my wife.'

'Only religious symbols permitted.'

'She is like an angel to me.'

They puzzled over this one for a while, then reluctantly admitted the picture. Not that I would be able to have anything as deadly as the original. It was whisked away and a photographic copy returned. Angelina seemed to be scowling in this print or perhaps that was only my imagination.

'All of your personal items, identification and so on will be returned to you when you leave,' I was coldly informed.

'While on Cliaand you will wear local dress and observe local customs. Your personal items are there.' Three very utilitarian and ugly pieces of luggage were indicated. 'Here is your identification card.' I grabbed at it, happy to be assured of my existence, still naked and beginning to get a chill.

'What is in this locked case?' an inspector called out, a ring of expectancy in his voice like that of a hound catching the scent. They all stopped work and came over as the incriminating case was held out for my inspection. Their expressions indicated that whatever answer I gave would be admission of crime to be followed by the death penalty. I permitted myself to cringe back and roll my eyes.

'Sirs, I have done nothing wrong . . .' I cried.

'What is it?'

'Military weapons—'

There were stifled cries and one of them looked around as though for a gun to execute me on the spot. I stammered on.

'But, sirs, you must understand. These are the reason I came to your hospitable planet. My firm, Fazzoletto-Mouchoir Ltd., is an old and much respected manufacturer in the field of military electronics. These are samples. Some most delicate. Only to be opened in the presence of an armament specialist.'

'I am armament specialist,' one of them said, stepping forward. I had noted him earlier because of his bald head and a sinister scar that drew up one eye in a perpetual wink.

'Pleased to meet you, sir. I am Pas Ratunkowy.' He was unimpressed by my name and did not offer his. 'If I can have my key ring I will open said case and display to you its contents.'

A camera was swung into place to record the entire operation, before I was permitted to proceed. I unlocked the case and flipped back the lid. The armament specialist glared down at the various components in their padded niches. I explained.

'My firm is the originator and sole manufacturer of the memory line of proximity fuses. No other line is as compact as ours, none as versatile.' I used tweezers to take a fuse from a holder. It was no larger than a pinhead. 'This is the most miniscule, designed to be used in a weapon as small as a handgun. Firing activates the fuse which will then detonate the charge in the slug when it comes near a target of predetermined size. This other fuse is the most intelligent, designed for use in heavy weapons or missiles.' They all leaned forward eagerly when I held up the wafer of the Mem-IV and pointed out its singular merits.

'All solid state construction, capable of resisting incredible pressures, thousands of G's, massive shocks. It can be preset to detonate only when approaching a specific target, or can be programmed externally and electronically at any time up to the moment of firing. It contains discrimination circuits that will prevent explosion in the vicinity of friendly equipment. It is indeed unique.'

I replaced it carefully and closed the lid on the case. A happy sigh swept through the spectators. This was the kind of thing they really *liked*. The armament specialist took up the case.

'This will be returned to you when it is needed to demonstrate.'

Reluctantly, the examination drew to a close. The fuses had been the highpoint of the search and nothing else could quite equal this. They had some fun squeezing the tubes and emptying the jars in my toilet kit but their hearts were not really in it. Finally tiring of this they bundled away all my goods and tossed me the new clothing.

'Four and a half minutes to dress,' an exiting inspector said. 'Bring bags.'

My garments were not what might be considered high fashion under any conditions. Underwear and such were a drab utilitarian gray and manufactured from some substance that felt like a mixture of shredded machine shop waste and sandpaper. I sighed and dressed. The outer garment was a one piece jumpsuit sort of thing that made me look like some giant form of wasp with its wide black and yellow bands. Well, if that is what the well dressed Cliaandian wore, that is what I would wear. Not that I had much choice. I picked up the two bags, their sharp handles cutting into my palms, and left through the single open door.

'Car,' a guard said outside, pointing to a driverless bubbletopped vehicle that stood nearby. We were now in a large room, still decorated in the same prison gray. The side door of the vehicle opened at my approach.

'I will be pleased to take car,' I nodded and smiled. 'But where shall I go—'

'Car knows. In.'

Not the galaxy's most witty conversationalists. I threw in my bags and sat down. The door wheezed shut and the bank of lights on the robotdriver lit up. We started forward and a heavy portal swung open before us. And another and another, each one thick enough to seal a bank vault. After the last one we shot up into the open air and I winced at the impact of sunlight. And looked with great interest at the passing scene.

Cliaand, if this nameless city was any example, was a modernized, mechanized, and busy world. Cars and heavy lorries filled the motorways, all apparently under robot control since they were evenly spaced and moved at impressive speeds. Pedways were on both sides and crossed overhead. There were stores, signs, crowds, uniforms. Uniforms! That single word does not convey the bemedaled and multicolored glories that surrounded me. *Everyone* wore a uniform of some sort with the different colors, I am sure, denoting the different branches and services. None of them were striped yellow and black. One more handicap placed in my way, but I shrugged it off. When you are drowning who cares if a teacup of water is poured over your head. Nothing about this piece of work was going to be easy.

My car darted out of the rushing traffic, dived down into another tunnel entrance and drew to a stop before an ornately decorated doorway. The great golden letters *Zlato-Zlato* were inscribed over the entrance which, in Cliaandian, might be described as *luxury*. This was a pleasant change. A beribboned, jeweled and elegant door-man rushed forward to open the door, then stopped and curled his lip when he saw my clothes. He let go of the door and stamped away and his place was taken by a bullet-necked individual in a dark gray uniform. Little silver crossed knife-and-battle-ax insignia were on both shoulders and his buttons were silver skulls. Somehow, not very encouraging.

'I am Pacov,' this depressing figure rumbled. 'Your bodyguard.'

'A pleasure to meet you, sir, a real pleasure.'

I climbed out, carrying my own bags it will be noted, and followed the grim back of my watchdog into the lobby of the hotel, which is what it proved to be. My identification was accepted with a maximum of discourtesy, a room assigned, a bellboy reluctantly prodded into showing me the way and off we went. My status as a theoretically respected offworld sales representative got me into the establishment, but that did not mean that I had to like it. My wasp colours branded me an alien, and alien they were going to keep me.

The quarters were luxurious, the bed soft, the bugs enthusiastically present. Sound and optic, they seemed to be built into every fitting and fixture. Every other knob on the knobbed furniture was a microphone and the light bulbs turned to follow me with their beady little eyes when I moved. When I went into the bathroom to shave an optical eye looked back at me through the lightly silvered mirror and there was another optical pickup in the end of my toothbrush – no doubt to spy out any secrets lurking in my molars. All very efficient.

They thought. It made me laugh, and I did, turning it into a snort when it emerged so my patient bodyguard would not be suspicious. He pad-padded after me wherever I went in the spacious apartment. No doubt he would sleep at the foot of my bed when I retired.

All of this was of no avail. Love laughs at locksmiths –

and so does Jim diGriz. Who knows an incredible amount, if you will excuse my seeming immodesty, about bugging. This was a case of massive overkill. So there were a lot of bugs. So what would you do with all that information? Computer circuitry would be completely useless in an observational situation like this one, which meant that a large staff of human beings would be watching, recording and analyzing. There is a limit to the number of people who can be assigned to this kind of work because a geometric progression soon takes place with watchers watching watchers until no one is doing anything else. I am sure there was a large staff keeping a keen eye on me, foreigners were rare enough to enjoy this luxury. Not only would my quarters be bugged but the areas I normally passed through, ground cars and such.

The entire city could *not* be bugged, nor was there reason to do so. All I had to do was act my normal humble, cover-role self for a while until I found the opportunity to leave the bugged areas. And cook up a plan that would permit my complete disappearance once I was out of sight. I would have only one chance at this; whatever plan I produced would have to work the first time out or I would be a very dead rat.

Pacov was always there, watching my every motion. He was watching when I went to sleep at night and the suspicious look in those hard little eyes was the first thing I saw in the morning. Which was just the way I wanted it. Pacov would be the first to go, but until then his mere presence with me meant that my watchers were relaxed. Let them relax. I looked relaxed, too – but I wasn't. I was examining every aspect of the city that I could see, looking for that rathole.

On the third day I found it. It was one of the many possibilities I had under consideration and it quickly proved to be the best. I made plans accordingly and that night smiled into the darkness as I went to sleep. I'm sure the smile was observed with infrared cameras – but what can be read from a smile?

The fourth day opened as did all the others with breakfast served in the room.

'My my, but I am hungry today,' I told the glowering Pacov. 'It must be the exhilarating atmosphere and aura of good cheer on your fine planet. I believe I will have a little more to eat.'

I did. A second breakfast. Since I had no idea when my next meal might be I decided to stoke up as best I could.

Standard routine followed. We emerged from the hotel at the appointed hour and the robotcar was waiting. It started at once towards its programmed destination, the war office where I had been demonstrating the effectiveness of the Fazzoletto-Mouchoir fuses. A number of targets had been destroyed, and today others would be blasted under even more exacting circumstances. It was all good fun.

We surfaced on the main road, spun down it and turned off into the side road that led to our destination. Traffic was light here – as always – and no pedestrians were in sight. Perfect. Street after street zipped by and I felt a familiar knot of tension developing. All or nothing, Slippery Jim, here we go . . .

'Ah-choo,' I said, with what I hoped was appropriate realism, and reached for my handkerchief. Pacov was suspicious. Pacov was always suspicious.

'Bit of dust in nose, you know how it is,' I said. 'Say, look, is that not the good General Trogbar over there?' I pointed with my free hand.

Pacov was well trained. His eyes only flickered aside for an instant before they returned to me. The instant was all I needed. Knotted into the handkerchief was a roll of small coins, the only weapon I could obtain under the authority's watchful gaze. I had assembled it, coin by coin, under the bedcovers at night. As the eyes flickered my hand struck, swinging the hard roll in a short arc that ended on the side of Pacov's head. He slumped with a muffled groan.

And even as he slumped down I was leaning over into the front of the car and banging down on the emergency stop button. The motor died, the brakes locked, we squealed to a stop and the doors popped open. Not more than a dozen paces from the selected spot. A bullseye. I was out and running at the same moment.

Because when I hit my bodyguard and the stop button every alarm must have lit up on the bugging board – there were plenty of little seeing eyes in the car. The forces of the enemy were launched at the same instant I was. All I had were seconds – a minute perhaps – of freedom before the troops closed in and grabbed me.

Would it be enough time?

Running, head down as fast as I could, I turned and skidded into the narrow opening of the service street. This cut through behind a row of buildings and emerged on a different street. There were robots here loading rubbish into bins, but they ignored me as I ran by since they were simple M types programmed for nothing but this kind of work.

The robot pusher was another matter. He was human and had an electronic lash that he used to stir the robots along. It cracked out and snapped around me and the electric current crackled into my side.

CHAPTER FIVE

IT WAS SHOCKING, to say the least, but I barely felt it. The voltage is kept low since it is meant to stir the robots, not to cook out their brain circuits. I grabbed the whip as soon as it hit and pulled hard.

All of this was of course according to plan. I had seen this robot pusher and his work gang in this same place every day when we passed; Cliaand does love its routine. The robot pusher, a thick-necked and thuggy looking individual, could be counted on to interfere with a running alien – and had done just as I had hoped. When I pulled on the whip I had him off balance and he staggered towards me, jaw agape, and I let him have a roundhouse right on the point of that agaping jaw. It connected.

He shook his head, growled something, and came at me with his hands ready to crunch and rend.

This was *not* according to plan. He was supposed to drop instantly so I could rush through the rest of the routine before the cavalry arrived. How could I have known that not only did he have the IQ of a block of stone but the constitution of one as well? I stepped aside, his fingers grabbed empty air, and I began to sweat. Time was passing and I had no time. I had to render this hulk unconscious in the quickest way possible.

I did. It wasn't graceful but it worked. I tripped him as he went by, then jumped on his back and rode him to the ground, accelerating his fall. And held him by the head and pounded it against the pavement. It took three good knocks – I was afraid the pavement would give way before he did – before he grunted and relaxed.

In the distance the first siren sounded. I sweated harder. Indifferent to the ways of men, the robots dumped their dustbins.

The robot pusher was dressed in a uniform of a decomposed green in color, no doubt symbolic of his trade. It was closed with a single zipper which I unzipped, then began to work the clothing off his bulky and unyielding form. While the sirens grew closer. At the last moment I had to stop and tear his boots off in order to remove the trousers, a noisome operation that added nothing good to the entire affair.

The siren echoed loudly from the walls of the service street and brakes squealed nastily close by.

With what very well might be called frantic haste I pulled the uniform on over my own wasp-like garb and zipped it shut. Running feet pounded loudly towards me. I grabbed up the whip and let the nearest robot have a crack right across his ball bearings.

'Stuff this man into a bin!' I ordered and stood back as it grabbed up its former master.

The feet had just vanished from view when the first of the red uniformed soldiers burst into sight.

'An alien!' I shouted, and shook my whip towards the other end of the narrow street. 'He went thataway. Fast. Before I could stop him.'

The soldiers kept going fast as well. Which was a good thing since the pair of recently removed boots were lying there right in plain sight. I threw them into the bin after their owner and cracked the whip on my half dozen robots.

'We march,' I ordered. 'To the next location.' I hoped they were programmed for a regular route – and they were. The truck-robot led the way and the others fell in behind him. I went behind, whip ready. My little procession emerged into the police gorged, soldier full street. Armored vehicles twisted around us and drivers cursed. My faithful band of robots struck straight across the street through this mess while I, with a paralyzed smile on my lips, trotted along after them. I was afraid that if I made any attempt to change the orders my mechanical team would stage a sitdown right there in the street. We passed behind the abandoned ground-car just as my old body-guard, Pacov, was being helped from it. I turned my back on him and tried to ignore the chill prickling up and down the nape of my neck. If he recognized me . . .

The first robot entered another serviceway and I staggered after them until, after what felt like a two day walk, I entered this haven of relative safety. It was a coolish day but I was sweating heavily: I leaned against the wall to recover while my robots emptied the bins. More cars were still appearing in the street I had so recently left and a flight of jets thundered by overhead. My, but they certainly were missing me.

What next? A good question. Very soon now, when no trace of the fugitive alien could be found, someone would remember the one witness to his escape. And they would want to talk to the robot pusher again. Before that moment came I would have to be elsewhere – but where? My assets were very limited; a collection of garbage collecting robots, now industriously clanking away at their trade, two uniforms – one worn over the other – either of which made me a marked man, and an electronic whip. Good only for whipping robots; the feeble current it generated was just enough to close a relay to cancel a previous order or action. What to do?

There was a grating noise close behind me and I jumped aside as a rusty iron door slid upwards. A fat man in a white hat poked his head out.

'I got another barrel in here for you, Slobodan,' he said, then looked suspiciously at me. 'You ain't Slobodan.'

'You're right. Slobodan is someone else. And he is somewhere else. In the hospital. Having a hernia removed. They're putting in a new one.'

Was opportunity tapping? I talked fast and thought even faster. There was still plenty of rushing about in the street I had so recently crossed but no one was looking into the serviceway. I cracked my whip across the gearbox of the nearest robot and ordered him to me.

'Follow that man,' I said, snapping my whip in the right direction. White hat popped back inside, the robot followed him and I followed the robot.

Into a kitchen. A big one, a restaurant kitchen obviously. And there was no one else in sight.

'What time do you open?' I asked. 'I'm getting quite an appetite on this job.'

'Not until tonight – hey! Tell this robot to stop following me and get that garbage out of here.'

The cook was backing around the room with the robot trundling faithfully after him. They made a fine pair.

'Robot,' I said, and cracked the whip. 'Do not follow that man any more. Just reach out your implacable little robot hands and grab him by the arms so he cannot get away.'

The robot's reflexes, being electronic, were faster than the cook's. The steel hands closed, the cook opened his mouth to complain – and I stuffed his hat into it. He chewed it angrily and made muffled noises deep in his throat. He kept this up all the time I was tying him into a chair with a fine assortment of towels, securing the gag in place as well. No one else had appeared and my luck was still running strong.

'Out,' I ordered the robot, cracking it across the patient metal back. The others were still working away and I laid about like a happy flagellant until they were all quivering for orders.

'Return. To the place from whence you came this morning. Go now.'

Like well trained troops they turned and started away. Thankfully, in the direction away from the street we had just crossed. I popped back into the kitchen and locked the door. Safe for the moment. They would trace me to the robot rubbishmen sooner or later, but would have no idea where or when I had left the convoy. Things were working out just fine.

The captive cook had managed to knock the chair over and was wriggling, chair and all, towards the exit.

'Naughty,' I said, and took the largest cleaver from the rack. He stopped at once and rolled his eyes at me. I put the cleaver and the whip where they could be reached quickly and looked about. For a little while at least I could breathe easy and make some definite plans. It had all been rush and improvise so far. There was a sudden knocking in the distance and the sharp ringing of a bell. I sighed and picked up the cleaver again. Rush and improvise was the motto of this operation.

'What is that?' I asked the cook, slipping the hat from his mouth for the moment.

'The front door. Someone there,' he said hoarsely, his eyes on the cleaver I held ready over his head. I restored the gag and sidled to the swinging door on the far wall and opened it enough to peek through.

The dining room beyond was dark and empty. The banging and ringing came from the entrance on the far side. No one else had appeared to answer this noisy summons so I felt safe in assuming that the cook and I were alone for the moment. Now to see what it was all about. With the cleaver at the ready I went to the front entrance, slid back the bolt and opened the door a crack.

'Whaddayawant?' I asked, aiming for the same rudimentary grammar and low accent voiced by the cook.

'Refrigerator service. You called you got trouble. What kind of trouble?'

'Big trouble!' My heart bounded with unexpected joy. 'Come in and bring biggest toolbox you got.'

It was a fair sized toolbox and I let him in, closed the door behind, and tapped him smartly on the back of the head with the flat of the cleaver blade. He folded nicely. His uniform was a utilitarian dark green, a great improvement on wasp, white or garbage, my only choice up to this moment. I stripped him quickly and tied him to a chair next to the cook where they commiserated in silence with each other. For the first time I was ahead of my pursuers. With luck it would be some hours before my captives were discovered and connected with my flight. I put the green uniform on, prepared a large number of sandwiches, picked up the toolbox, tipped my uniform cap to the captives in the kitchen, and slipped out the front door.

A large riding robot was standing there, another toolbox hanging from one hand, humming quietly to itself. Painted on its metallic chest was the same crest of the service company that now adorned my own chest.

'We travel in comfort,' I said. 'Take this.' I got my fingers out of the way just in time as it reached for the toolbox.

During my rapid trips through the city I had seen a number of these riding robots from a distance, but had never been close to one before. There was a sort of saddle arrangement on their backs where the operator rode, but I hadn't the slightest idea of how to get into the seat. Did the thing kneel to be mounted or drop down a ladder or what? Cars and other robots were going by in this street and a squad of soldiers was approaching at a good clip. I found myself sweating again.

'I wish to leave. Now.'

Nothing happened. Except that the soldiers were that much closer. The robot stood as stolid as a statue. There was no help here. I didn't know if it was the orthodox manner or not, I had to do something, so I put one foot on the thing's hip socket, grabbed a riding light up near its shoulder blade and swarmed up its side. Hidden motors hummed louder as it shifted balance to accommodate my added weight. I slipped into the saddle just as the squad of soldiers trotted by. They ignored me completely.

The seat was comfortable. I had a good view, with my head at least three meters above the ground, and I hadn't the slightest idea what to do next. Though leaving this vicinity would make fine openers. A compact control panel was set into the top of the robot's head and I pressed the button labeled WALK. I felt the grinding vibration of internal gears being engaged and it began to mark time in place. A good beginning. A rapid search found the button marked FORWARD. It lurched ahead and broke into an easy trot. I soon left the police and all the excitement behind.

A plan was needed. I rode my mechanical mount through the heart of the city and considered my position. One man against a world. Very poetic and possibly disconcerting except for the fact that I had been in this position before while they had not. All of the security arrangements meant that aliens were few and far between on Cliaand and always kept under close surveillance. Perhaps they had never lost track of one before and this was sure to be a great annoyance. Heads would roll. Fine. As long as one of them wasn't mine. In a sense I had the advantage. Other than my cover identity they knew nothing about me. If I could lose myself in the depths of their depressing culture I would be impossible to find. As long as I stayed submerged. Positive action would come later. Right now I had to save my valuable hide and plan for the future.

44

One of the city exits was ahead and an unusually large number of uniformed individuals were involved in examining and searching everyone attempting to leave. A touch on the LEFT button started my mount down another street away from this danger. When I wanted to leave the city I would. That time had not yet arrived.

By mid afternoon I had a working knowledge of the layout of the city and was developing callouses on my bottom. The robot was going slower and evidently in need of a recharge from some handy wall socket. I needed a recharge from the sandwiches in the toolbox. We both needed a rest. And the chances were good that my prisoners had been found in the kitchen and that the new alarm was going out. Using the more vacant side streets I worked the robot back to the manufacturing district that I had noted earlier and looked for a place to hole up. I had seen some factories and warehouses with a distinctly deserted air that would fit my needs.

One did. Cobwebs on the windows and rust on the hinges of the front door. No one in sight and a lock that I could have opened in the dark with my fingernails. The door creaked open, not a soul was in sight. We slipped in and the bolt clicked behind us. Security. The place was deserted, dusty and for the most part empty. A great ancient piece of machinery brooded in one corner, as featureless and mysterious as a lost jungle idol, with sacrifices of discarded cartons about its feet. Perfect. I lunched, relaxed, searched the building, found an interior room with no windows, brought in the flashlight and a pencil from the toolbox and one of the sacrificial cartons. Time for the next step.

Pencil in hand, the blank square before me illuminated by the light, I spoke aloud.

'Now hear this. Memory is about to begin. The count will start at ten. I will become tired during the progression and by the time zero is reached I will be asleep. The memory is keyed to the word . . . xanadu!'

'Ten,' I said, feeling fine. Then 'Nine' and I yawned. By the time I hit five my eyelids were drooping and I have no memory at all of ever getting to zero.

CHAPTER SIX

I AWOKE TO FIND MY FINGERS STIFF, my arm cramped, my eyes sore. And the great square of cardboard covered with a complex wiring diagram. The subconscious is a fine place to hide things unknown to the conscious mind. I not only had the diagram but suddenly realized that I now knew just how to use it. The plan was a dazzlingly simple one and I was instantly jealous of whoever dreamed it up. It also required a bit of time, a lot of electronic wiring and equipment. All of which would have to be stolen. I sighed and stretched my cramped muscles. It had been a tiring day and my sleep during the hypnotic trance had been no sleep at all. Tomorrow would be another day, the pace of pursuit should have died down.

Tomorrow and tomorrow were nothing but work. I was a stainless steel rat gone to ground and there was much scuttling about to be done. The city continued in its business around me, and I'm sure the search for me went on unabated although it never came near my cozy retreat. I soldered and wired, stole food and other items of comfort and luxury in an almost offhand way. Cliaand seemed to have a very low level of crime because almost no precautions appeared to have been taken to prevent the sort of burglary I indulged in. Either the criminal class had all been killed off or they now ran the government. Which could very likely be the case. My solitary period would end soon and I would abandon my passive role and indulge in the espionage that I had been sent here to do.

Leaving the city was far simpler than I had imagined. By

adroit loitering in the area of the checkpoint I saw that the military were in charge of the operation which appeared to proceed in a very simpleminded and military way. A certain amount of saluting and ordering, examining of papers and rubber stamping, a quick search and away. I hoped it would work that easily for me. To make the entire operation military I stole an army truck at dusk, stopping it by planting my robot in the road in front of it. The truck vibrated to a stop and the driver put his head out and cursed fluently. Most of the words had not been in my language lessons and I filed them for future use. He seemed to be alone, which was a blessing.

'And the same to you,' I told him. 'That is no way to talk to civilians. This is emergency.'

'What emergency?' Suspiciously.

'This emergency.' Enthusiastically.

The needle slammed home in the side of his neck and he slumped. I had also made a raid on a chemical supply house. I pushed him aside, put on his uniform cap, ordered the robot into the back of the truck and returned to the warehouse for my wares. They stowed neatly behind the crates of dehydrated meals, forms in triplicate, cans of boot polish and other essential military items in the truck. Dressed in the soldier's red uniform, he dozing nicely in my green, I said good-bye to the robot, my only friend on this inhospitable planet. He answered nothing in return which did not hurt me. I left.

My papers and identification were accepted with military taciturnity, examined and approved, and I was free. I sped merrily out into the night and phase two of my plan. Physically this involved a lot of rushing about, stealing various vehicles to confuse my trail, and a long trek through the central desert to a certain landmark. This was a great lump of stone standing very much by itself in the sea of sand. It was shaped very much like a pot and was called *Ionac* in the Cliaand language. Which means *pot* and gives you some idea of the great scope of their imagination. The camouflage net covered the stolen groundcar, and I worked most industriously here for seven full days before I was satisfied with the results. What I had built, with my own two little hands and the help of an excavation robot, was a completely selfcontained underground shelter no more than a 100 meters from Pot rock. This was the last and final bit of preparation for phase three. That night I initiated this phase. My little home-wired transmitter was tuned and ready to go, the antenna pointed straight up at the zenith. Exactly at midnight I turned it on and the narrow, highly directional signal blasted up into space. I kept it going for exactly thirty seconds, then shut it off.

That was that. The die cast and the next move was up to Them. Them being a Special Corps detachment that had arranged this phase. Hopefully arranged it. I would know nothing positive until the following evening. If the plan worked, and I chewed my lip a little over the *if* as I stowed the radio back into the car, my signal should have been received by them – and only by them. Narrow band width and very directional. Impossible to detect. The Cliaandians should know nothing about it at all. But great powers would have been set into motion. Mighty computers computed and gigantic rockets fired. A selected meteorite set into motion along with a collection of accompanying space debris. Out in space beyond the Cliaand detectors. But coming this way, aimed at the solitary rock of the Pot. I had a day and a night to wait.

Knowing my attitude towards unproductive waiting I had arranged a little party for myself. There was good food, or as good as I could get in preserved rations, and better drink since I had a far wider assortment to select from. Wine with the meal and more potent distillates afterward. For closers I lit a cigar and turned on the pocket-sized screen of the

mini-projector and ran a couple of the feelthy-feelthy-film
that I had bought at an army exchange. Pretty crude stu
for the troops, though it looked pretty attractive to me i
my desert nomad role. Sleep lowered its gentle blanket, da
followed night and then night again in its turn. And a
soon as it was dark I was out there with my field glasse
quartering the sky. Nothing. It wasn't due for hours yet, bu
I was impatient. The entire plan was beginning to soun
absurd. And I was feeling very much alone, trapped on thi
alien planet light years from civilization. The mood was
depressing one. I had a drink from my pocket flash.

If all were going well the great hunk of rock should b
heading toward Cliaand on a collision course. When it wa
detected by the defenses it should be considered as jus
another piece of spatial debris. It would hit the atmospher
and burn. If they were tracking it, on the offchance that i
might be more than it appeared, this should reassure them
The speed and temperature ruled out any living cargo. I
should also be a little difficult to follow because of th
accompanying debris that would also be bouncing bac
radar signals. The meteor would burn through the atmo
sphere and hit the desert with an impact enough t
destroy anything living. If there were an investigation i
would be dilatory, and important things would happe
before the investigators arrived. I hoped. It all sounded s
good in theory and seemed such an absurd piece of madnes
in practice.

Very close to midnight a new star flickered and burne
in the clear sky above and I sighed and put away the flask
Right on time like a commuter rocket. The point grew
brighter and brighter, then brighter still. Aimed right a
me. I knew that computers and astronomers were good
but not that good. Was the thing going to come down righ
on top of me?

Not quite. As I watched it appeared to drift to one side

accelerating as it went, while a great hissing roar like a heavenly steam kettle crackled through the air. I jumped into the groundcar and kicked it to life as the burning bomb of light vanished behind the tower of the Pot to be followed instantly by a rolling explosion that lit the night air and outlined the Pot with fire. I moved.

My headlights picked out a raw spot in the ground, surrounded by debris and overhung with a cloud of smoke and dust. And at the bottom was the great glazed chunk of steaming rock. Bullseye! I backed the car behind the nearest sand dune and thumped the transmitter. There was another explosion, infinitely smaller than the one of impact, and pieces of rock zinged above my head. When I next looked at the meteor it had been neatly cracked in half by the charges and the jelly-like liquid that had protected the contents was soaking into the sand.

At the same moment I heard the rising rumble of approaching jets and killed the headlights. They roared by overhead, triangles of darkness against the stars, and tilted into a turn. At this moment I gained new appreciation of the Cliaand powers of suspicion as well as a deep respect for their radar, computers and organization. I was going to have less time than I thought. I jumped into the hole trying to ignore the heat of the crackling rock.

The equipment was intact, sealed into flat boxes, and there was just enough light from the stars for me to drag them out and stow them into the car. The jets circled above, brought to the general area by radar triangulation and searching now for the precise point of impact. Not that they could see much, at their speed in the darkness. But slower aircraft were undoubtedly on the way. With instrumentation and lights that could quarter the area. I moved a little faster at the thought, my imagination already producing the flutter of great propellers on the horizon. Panting heavily, the last box in the groundcar, I waited until the jets were swinging away from me before starting for my hidey-hole. I went as fast as I dared, steering around the bigger obstacles and bumping over the small. When the jets were swung in my direction I stopped, trying to think tiny, waiting for them to pass. On the next rush I made it to the entrance. As I dropped the first of the boxes into the hole in the ground I *did* hear engines. Strong lights were flickering in the distance – coming my way. Things were being shaved entirely too close. I hurled the boxes out one after another, not caring where or how they landed. I was ready to dive after them and stow them carefully, when great wings fluttered overhead and a sizzling light raced from beneath the Pot and flashed over, blinding me.

It moved on and I groped for the car's starting switch through a galaxy of rainbows and roaring discs of light. The groundcar started up, then leaped into motion as I kicked it into gear. As the light hit again I fell over the side and lay still.

For a considerable length of time I was motionless and bathed by the light, searing in even through my closed eyelids. It felt as though I lay there between two and three years, but it could only have been a fraction of a second. The ladder was in place and I climbed down it, barking my shins well on the tumbled clutter of boxes. Rooting about like a mole in the darkness I kicked and pushed them through the entranceway ahead of me. The roar of great machines was loud behind me, joined a moment later by the sound of rapid firing weapons and the boom of explosions.

'Perfect,' I panted, hurling the last of the boxes. 'Weapons are meant to be used, so they are using them. I was sure they would be a trigger-happy bunch and I'm most pleased to see my conclusions justified.' A louder boom announced the destruction of my car. It could not have been better. I felt for the transmitter by the entrance and took it with me as I climbed up the ladder, at a much more leisurely pace.

Standing comfortably on the ladder, with my elbows resting on the ground, I had the best seat for the performance. Jets roared and propellers thrashed from the sky above. Bullets sang and bombs exploded. The groundcar burned nicely, sending up angry spurts of flame whenever the wreck was strafed. As the banging and booming began to taper off I livened it up by pressing the first button on the transmitter.

With a satisfying explosion of sound the rapidfire guns began to fire from the top of the Pot, while at occasional intervals rockets shot up out of the launcher. Every other round was tracer so the show was most impressive. The forces in the sky zoomed away to regroup, then returned to the attack with savage vigor. The top of the Pot and the ground all around was torn with explosions. I had raided the Cliaand armory for my weapons and it was nice to see the same side shooting at itself. A bomb exploded no more than thirty meters from me and sand shook down my neck. This part of the show was over; time for the finale.

Sand was falling all around me as I dropped back to the bottom of the hole. With a certain amount of haste I pulled the ladder through the entrance, then tugged on the cables and darted inside. A good part of the sand I had dug out was piled above the entrance and held back by restraining boards. Now removed, I pushed the door shut as the sand slid down with sudden speed. Standing there in the darkness I counted slowly to ten to allow time for the sandslide to completely fill the hole. Then I pressed the second button.

Nothing happened.

And this was an essential part of the operation. With all the bombs going off, the ground still shook with their vibration, one more explosion would not be noticed. The second button was to have triggered a buried charge that would conceal all signs of my activities and seal my rat hole at the same time. If it did not go off I would be easily found and dug out . . .

Memory returned and I cursed my own foolishness. Of course I had made plans for this contingency. The radio signal from my little transmitter could not reach through the ground, I had known that. I groped for the flashlight I had left by the entrance, turned it on and saw the bare end of wire sticking through the wall. It was even labeled 2 so there would be no confusion if I were in a hurry.

I was in a hurry. The explosions were dying away, presumably the mechanical enemy on the Pot had been destroyed, and if my explosion did not go off soon it would look very suspicious to say the least. I wrapped the end of the wire, it extended up to ground level, around the whip aerial on the transmitter and thumbed the button again. There was silence.

Until a jarring explosion went off just overhead, shaking the bones inside my body and rattling my teeth together. My concrete cave boomed like a drum and dirt and chips rattled down. I was safe.

Snug as a roach in the rafters. I turned on the light and looked with pride on my residence for the next couple of weeks. Power supply, shielded of course, food, water, atmosphere renewal, everything a man might need. And the solid state circuity and devices that had arrived in the meteor. I would work and assemble my equipment and emerge ready to face the world. While the desert above was searched and quartered and the chase went further away. They would never think to look right under their noses, never! I smiled and looked for a bottle to open to celebrate.

CHAPTER SEVEN

NO LONGER A THIEF I, nor a hider under rocks. On the 13th day I had unblocked my door and dug my way back to the surface. With this symbolic act I left behind my fugitive's existence and entered Cliaandian society. With assorted identification and various uniforms I now played a wide selection of roles in this rather repellant society until I knew far more about it than I really cared. In my various identities I only brushed the periphery of the military since I wanted to save my energies for a frontal assault there in full power.

With this possibility I boarded an SST flight to Dosadan-Glup, the fair sized provincial city that happened to be situated adjacent to the military base of Glupost. From what I had been able to determine Glupost was also a major spaceship center and staging area for offworld expeditions. So there was more than chance to the fact that I loitered near enough to the seat reservation clerk to see who got what, and then asked for a seat next to a very attractive who.

Attractive only to me, I hasten to add. By any other standard of measurement the flight-major would win no prizes. His jaw was too big, apparently designed to project into places where it wasn't wanted, and it had a nasty little cleft built into it as though it had cracked from being poked too far. Suspicious dark eyes lurked under simian shelving brows and the cavernous nostrils were twin furlined subway tunnels. I could not care less. I saw only the black uniform of the Space Armada, the many decorations signifying active service, and the wings-and-rockets of a senior pilot. He was my man.

'Good evening, sir, good evening,' I said as I slipped into the seat next to him. 'A pleasure to travel with you.'

He aimed the twin cannons of his nose at me and fired a broadside snort that signaled a close to the recently opened conversation. I smiled in return and buckled my belt and was slammed back into the cushions as the SST hurled itself into the night sky. At cruising altitude most of the wing area slipped back into the hull and I took out my pocket flask and detached the two small cups.

'It would be a pleasure to offer you a drink of refreshment, noble flight-major, in gratitude for your many services rendered to the glorious cause of Cliaand.'

This time he did not even bother to grunt, but instead picked at his teeth with a none too clean pinky nail until he extracted a fragment of meat from his recent dinner. Close examination convinced him that it was too large to discard so he reingested it with a certain relish. A man of simple pleasures. I offered a better one.

'Nothing too good for our boys in the service. This is narcolethe.' I sipped at the cup and smacked my lips.

He looked directly at me for the first time and there should have been little splintering sounds as his lips moved slowly into an unaccustomed smile.

'I'll drink that,' he said in a grating voice, and well he should since the small flask of liqueur would have cost him a month's salary. Narcolethe, the finest drink known to mankind, distilled in small quantities from a scarce botanical source on a minor planet at the galaxy's rim. Soothing, charming, subtle, intoxicating, inspiring, aphrodisiac, stimulating. It was everything any other drink was, plus much more, with no side effects and no hangover. He took the proffered cup and lowered the caverns of his nose over it and sipped.

'Not bad,' he said, and I smiled at this crude under-statement as though it were sincerest flattery and offered him the false name I had assumed. He thought about it and realized that an exchange was in order.

'Flight-Major Vaska Hulja.'

'The pleasure is mine, sir, the pleasure is mine. May I top that up for you, these cups are so small.'

Very soon, as our razor nosed craft cracked the sound barrier and boomed through the sleep of the dozing citizens on the ground, I came to almost love the flight-major. He was perfect, all-around, with no bulges of doubt or pock-marks of uncertainty. Just as a spider is a perfect spider or a vampire bat a perfect vampire bat, he was a perfect free-wheeling bastard. As his spirits lifted and his tongue grew thick the anecdotes became more detailed. The flight-major on strafing:

'Never make mistake of going after individuals or small groups, it is overall effect that counts. Stay to plan, hit buildings and grouped vehicles, finish the run. On a second run it's all right to hit groups of people, but only big ones, with firebombs. That spreads and splatters and gets the most.'

The flight-major on recreation:

'There was just the two of us and we had maybe a dozen bottles and case of weedstick, enough for couple of days, so we got these three girls, one as a spare, you know, just in case, and took them . . .'

The flight-major on off-worlders:

'Animals. You can't tell me we can even interbreed with them. Obvious that Cliaand is source of all intelligent life in universe and only civilizing influence.'

There was more like this and I could only nod my head in rapt attention. Perfect, as I said. What had me almost pulsating with joy was the information that he had just been assigned to the Glupost station after his R & R. This was his first visit to the immense base after years of duty on the fighting front. Destiny was controlling the fall of the dice.

What I had to do next was dangerous and involved a great deal of risk – but the opportunity presented was too good to miss. In the weeks that I had been exploring the details of Cliaand society I had come to know it in great depth. I thought. Now was the time to find out how much I really did know. For the part of society I had picked my way through was just the periphery, the non-military part and the military was the one that really counted. It dominated this world in every way and had managed to extend its dominance to other worlds as well. Despite the rules of logic, the inverse square, and history. I was going to have to apply my little bit of know-how to crack the final barrier.

I was joining the army. Enlisting in the Space Armada. With the rank of flight-major. As the ship tilted into its landing approach I put thought into deed.

'Must you report to duty at once, Vaska?' Strong drink had put us on a first name basis. He shook his head in a shaggy *no*.

'Tomorrow I am due.'

'Wonderful. You do not wish to spend your last night of leave between the cold sheets of a solitary bed in the B.O.Q. Just think what else could be accomplished in the same time.'

I went into some imaginary detail of what could be done with silken sheets in an unsolitary bed. Good food and fine drink were mentioned as well, but these were only of contingent interest. The flask tilted once more and he nodded cheerful agreement to my plan.

As soon as we had landed and our baggage had been disgorged, a robocab took us to the Dosadan-Glup Robotnik. This was the local branch of a planet-wide chain of hotels that specialized in non-human service. Everything was mechanized and computerized. Human beings presumably visited them once in a while to check the gauges and empty the tills, but I had never seen one although I had used these hotels quite often, for many obvious reasons. I had occasionally seen other guests entering or leaving but we had avoided each other like plague carriers. The Robotniks were islands of privacy in a sea of staring eyes. They had certain drawbacks, but I had long since learned to cope with these. To the Robotnik we went.

The front door opened automatically when we approached and a sort of motorized-dolly robot slipped out of its kennel and sang to us.

'World famous since the day we opened,
The Dosadan-Glup Robotnik welcomes you.
I am here to take your luggage—
Order me and I'll help you!'

This was sung in a rich contralto voice to the accompaniment of a 200 piece brass band; a standard recording of all the Robotnik hotels. I hated it. I kicked the robot back, it was pressing close to our ankles, and pointed to the robocar

'Luggage. There. Five pieces. Fetch.'

It hummed away and plunged eager tentacles into the cab. We entered the hotel.

'Don't we have four pieces luggage?' Vaska asked, frowning those beetling eyebrows in thought.

'You're right, I must have miscounted.' The luggage robot caught up and passed us, with our suitcases and the back seat torn out of the cab. 'We have five now.'

'Good evening . . . gentlemen,' the robot at the desk murmured, with a certain hesitation before the final word as it counted us and compared profiles in its memory bank. 'How may we serve you?'

'The best suite in the house,' I said as I signed a fictitious name and address and began to feed *boginje* bills into the pay slot on the desk. Cash in advance was the rule at the Robotnik with any balance returned upon departure. A bellboy robot, armed with a key, rolled out and showed us the way, throwing the door wide with a blare of recorded trumpets as though it were announcing the second coming.

'Very nice,' I said and pressed the button labeled *tip* on its chest which automatically deducted two *boginjes* from my credit balance.

'Order us some drinks and food,' I told the flight-major, pointing to the menu built into the wall. 'Anything you wish as long as there are steaks and champagne.'

He liked that idea and he was busily pushing buttons while I arranged the luggage. I also had a bug-detector strapped to my wrist which led me unerringly to the single optic-sonic bug. It was in the same place as every other one I had found, these hotels were really standardized, and I managed to move a chair in front of it when I opened my suitcase.

The delivery doors dilated and champagne and chilled glasses slid out. Vaska was still ordering away on the buttons and my credit balance, displayed in large numbers on the wall, was rolling rapidly backwards. I cracked the bottle, bouncing the cork off the wall near him to draw his inebriated attention, and filled the glasses.

'Let us drink to the Space Armada,' I said, handing him his glass and letting the little green pellet fall into it at the same time.

'To Space Armada,' he said, draining the glass and breaking into some dreary chauvinistic song that I knew I would have to learn, all about shining blast-tubes, gleaming guns, men of valor, burning suns. I'd had enough of it even before he began.

'You look tired,' I told him. 'Aren't you sleepy?'

'Sleepy . . . ' he agreed, his head bobbing.

'I think it would be a good idea for you to lie down on the bed and get some rest before dinner.'

'Lie down . . .' His glass fell to the rug and he stumbled across the room and sprawled full length on the nearest bed.

'See, you were tired. Go to sleep and I'll wake you later.'

Obedient to the hypnodrug, he closed his eyes and began snoring at once. If anyone were listening at the bug they would detect nothing wrong.

Dinner arrived, enough food to feed a squad – my money meant nothing to good old Vaska – and I ate a bit of steak and salad before going to work. I snapped open the kit and spread out the materials and tools.

The first thing was of course an injection that acted as a nerve block and numbed all sensation in my face. As soon as this took effect I propped the snoring flight-major up and trained the reading light full in his face. This would not be a hard job at all. We both had about the same bony structure and build, and the resemblance did not have to be perfect. Just close enough to match the prison-camp picture on his ID card. The quality of this picture was what one learns to expect from an identification photo, looking more like a shaven ape than a human.

The chin was the biggest job in every sense and massive injections of plastic jell built mine up to Vaska's heroic size. I molded its shape before it set, cleft and all, then went to work on the eyebrows. More plastic built up the brow ridges, and implanted black artificial hair drove home the resemblance. Contact lenses matched the color of his eyes and expanding rings in my nostrils flared them to the original's cave-like size. All that remained then was to transfer his fingerprints to the skintight and invisible plastic that covered my own fingers. Nothing to it.

While I altered Vaska's best uniform to a better fit for me he rose – as instructed – and ate some of the cold dinner. Sleep overcame him soon after that and this time he retired to the bed in the other room where his snores and grumbles would not annoy me.

I mixed a stiff drink and retired early. The morrow would be a busy day in my new identity. I was going into the Space Armada.

With a little luck I might get a clue as to the nature of their remarkable military powers.

CHAPTER EIGHT

'I'M SORRY, SIR, but you can't get in,' the guard in front of the gate said. The gate itself was made of riveted steel and was solidly set into a high stone wall capped with many strands of barbed wire.

'What do you mean I *can't* get in? I have been *ordered* to Glupost,' I shouted in my best military-obnoxious manner. 'Now press that button or whatever else you do to unlock that thing.'

'I can't open it, sir, the base is sealed from the outside. I'm stationed with the outside guard detail.'

'I want to see your superior officer.'

'Here I am,' a cold voice said in my ear. 'What is this disturbance?'

When I turned around I looked at his lieutenant's bar and he looked at my flight-major's double cross and I won that argument. He led me to the guardhouse and there was a lot of calling back and forth on the TV phone until he handed it to me and I looked a steely-eyed colonel in the face. I had already lost this argument.

'The base is sealed, flight-major,' he said.

'I have orders to report here, sir.'

'You were to report here yesterday. You have overstayed your leave.'

'I'm sorry, sir, must have been an error in recording. My orders read report today.' I held them up and saw that the reporting date *was* the previous day. That drunkard Vaska had got me into the trouble he deserved himself. The colonel smiled with all the sweetness of a king cobra in rut.

'If the mistake were in the orders, flight-major, there would certainly be no difficulty. Since the mistake was yours, *lieutenant*, we know where the error lies. Report to the security entrance.'

I hung up the phone and the guard lieutenant, grinning evilly, handed me a set of lieutenant's bars. I unclipped my double-crosses and accepted the humbler rank. I hoped promotion was as fast as demotion in the Space Armada. A guard detail marched me along the wall to a similar airlock type of entrance and I was passed through. My credentials and orders were examined, my fingerprints taken, and in a few minutes I was through the last gate and inside the base of Glupost.

A car was summoned, a private soldier took my bags, we drove to the officers' quarters and I was shown to my room. And all the time I kept my eyes open. Not that there was anything fascinating to see. See one military base and you've seen them all. Buildings, tents, chaps in uniform doing repetitive jumping, heavy expensive equipment all painted the same color, that sort of thing. What I had to find out would not be that easy to uncover. My bags were dumped in the tiny room, salutes exchanged, the soldier left, and a voice spoke hoarsely from the other bed.

'You don't happen to have a drink on you, do you?'

I looked closely and saw that what I at first thought was a bundle of crumpled blankets now appeared to contain a scrawny individual who wore dark glasses. The effort of talking must have exhausted him and he groaned, adding another breath of alcoholic vapor to the already rich atmosphere of the room.

'It so happens that I do,' I said, opening the window. 'My name is Vaska. Do you prefer any particular brand?'

'Ostrov.'

I could think of no drink by that title so presumably it was my roommate's name. Taking the flask with the most

64

potent beverage from my collection I poured him half a glass. He seized it with trembling fingers and drained it while shudders racked his frame. It must have done some good because he sat up in bed and held out the glass for more.

'We blast off in two days,' he said, sniffing the drink. 'This really isn't paint remover, is it?'

'No, it just smells that way to fool the MP's. Where to?'

'Don't make jokes so early in the morning. You know we never know what planet we're hitting. Security. Or are you with security?'

He blinked suspiciously in my direction: I would have to watch the questions until I knew more. I forced a smile and poured a drink for myself.

'A joke. I don't feel so good myself. I woke up a flight-major this morning . . .'

'And now you're a lieutenant. Easy come, easy go.'

'They didn't come that easy!'

'Sorry. Figure of speech. I've always been a lieutenant so I wouldn't know how the others feel. You couldn't just tip a little more into this glass? Then I'll be able to dress and we can get over to the club and get into some serious drinking. It's going to be awful, all those weeks without drink until we get back.'

Another fact. The Cliaand fought their battles refreshed with water. I wondered if I could. I sipped and the disturbing thought that had been poking at me for some minutes surfaced.

The real Vaska Hulja was back at the hotel and would be discovered. And I could do nothing about it because I was in this sealed base.

Some of the drink went down the wrong pipe and I coughed and Ostrov beat me on the back.

'I think it really is paint remover,' he said gloomily when I had stopped gasping, and began to dress.

65

As we walked to the officers' club I was in no mood for communication, which Ostrov probably blamed on my recent demotion. What to do? Drink seemed to be in order, it wasn't noon yet, and it would be wisest to wait until evening to crack out of the base. Face the problems as they arose. Right now I was in a perfect position to imbibe drink with my new peer group and gather information at the same time. Which, after all, was the reason that I was here in the first place. Before leaving I had slipped a tube of killalc pills into my pocket. One of these every two hours would produce a massive heartburn, but would also grab onto and neutralize most of the alcohol as soon as it hit the stomach. I would drink deep and listen. And stay sober. As we walked through the garish doorway of the club I slipped one out and swallowed it.

It was all rather depressing, particularly since I was sloshing the stuff down my throat as fast as I could drink it and buying rounds for the others and not feeling it at all. As the afternoon went on and thirsts increased other officers appeared in the club and there were soon a dozen other pilots crowded around our free-spending table. All drinking well and saying little of any interest.

'Drink, drink,' I insisted. 'Won it gambling. Don't need it where we're going,' and bought another round.

There was a great deal said, as one might well imagine, about the flying characteristics of various ships and I filed all the relevant details. And much mumbling over old campaigns, I dived from 50,000, planted the bombs, pulled up and that sort of thing. The only thing remarkable about all this was the unsullied record of victories. I knew the Cliaand armed forces were good, but looking at this collection of drunks almost made it impossible to believe they could be *that* good. But apparently they were. There were endless boasting tales of victory after victory and nothing else, and after a period I too came to believe.

These boys were good and the Space Armada of Cliaand a winner. It was all too depressing. By evening there was a literal falling away of the original drinkers, though their places at the table were filled quickly enough. When one of them slid to the floor the servants would gently carry him off. I realized that I was the last of the originals so no one would notice if I also made an exit in this apparently traditional manner. Letting my eyes close I sank deep into my chair, hoping this would do since I did not relish a trip to the debris littered floor. It took them some minutes to notice I was no longer functioning, but eventually they did. Hard hands caught at my knees and armpits and I was hauled off.

When the footsteps had rattled away I opened my eyes to a sort of dim chamber whose walls were lined with bunks. Nearby me was the gaping O of Ostrov's mouth, snoring away in his cups. As were the others. No one noticed when I pulled on my gloves and went to the door that opened into the company street and let myself out. It was almost dark and I had to leave the camp and I had not the slightest idea of how I could do it.

The gates were impossible. I strolled along the wall to the first one. Sealed and bolted shut, solid steel, with a brace of guards to see that the locks weren't tampered with. I walked on. There were guards every hundred paces or so along the wall and I assumed that there were an equal or greater number of electronic safeguards as well. As evening approached searchlights were turned on that illuminated the outside of the walls and glinted from the barbed wire that topped it. Admittedly all this was to keep anyone from getting in – but it worked equally well in the opposite direction. I walked on, trying to fight off the black depression that still threatened to overwehlm me. I passed through a medium sized atmosphere craft area, two runways and some hangars, with a collection of lumbering jet transports standing about. For a moment I considered stealing one of these – but where would I land without being captured? I had to be in this city tonight, not zipping off to parts unknown.

Beyond the aircraft was a high chain metal fence that cut off the spaceship area. Getting in there would be easy enough – but what would it accomplish? I could see the same high outer wall stretching off into the distance. There was a rumble in the sky and bright lights lanced down. I turned around and watched, sunk in gloom, as a delta wing fighter settled in heavily for a landing. It looked like one of the same type that had strafed me at Pot rock. The tires squealed when it was hit and the jets roared with reverse thrust – and I was running forward even while the idea was half-formed in my mind.

Madness? Perhaps. But in my line of business, crookery, you learn to rely on hunches and trained reflexes. And while I ran the parts all fell into place and I saw that this was It. Sweet, fast, clean and dangerous. The way I liked things. I took a false moustache out of my pocket and fixed it on my lip as I ran.

The jet turned and taxied off to a hardstand and I trotted after it. A car came out to meet it and a crew of mechanics began to service the jet. One of them unloaded a ladder and placed it next to the cockpit as the top of the canopy opened like an alligator's mouth. I ran a little faster as the pilot climbed down and made for the car. He was just climbing in when I came stumbling up and he returned my salute. A burly individual in heavy flying gear, the golden crescent of a major on his collar.

'Excuse me, sir,' I gasped, 'but the commandant asked me to make sure you had your papers.'

'What the hell are you talking about?' he grumbled, sliding into his seat. He sounded tired. I climbed into the back.

'Then you *don't* know. Oh, God! Driver – get going as fast as possible.'

The driver did, since that was his job, and I slipped the tube out of the holder in my hip pocket. When we were out of sight of the jet I raised it to my lips.

'Major . . .' I said, and he turned his head and grunted. I puffed.

He grunted again and raised his hand towards the little dart stuck in his cheek – then slumped forward. I caught him before he fell.

'Driver – stop! Something has happened to the major.'

The driver, obviously not a man of much imagination, took a quick look at the slumped figure and hit the brake. As soon as we skidded to a stop, I let him have a second narco-dart and he went off to join the major in dreamland. I laid them both on the ground and stripped off the officer's flying suit and helmet. With a little bit of struggling I managed to pull the things over my own uniform, then strapped on the helmet and pulled the tinted goggles down over my eyes. All of this took less than a minute. I left the dozing pair in each other's arms and headed the car back to the plane. So far so good. But this had been the easiest part. I stood on the brakes and skidded to a stop on the hardstand.

'Emergency!' I shouted, leaping from the car and running to the ladder. 'Unhook this thing so I can take off.'

The mechanics merely gaped at me, making no move towards the umbilical wires and hoses that connected the plane to the servicing pit. I wheeled the nearest one about and used the toe of my boot to move him in the right direction. He got the message clearly and the others now understood as well. They went to work. All except a grizzled noncom with a sleeve covered with hashmarks and stripes and a face covered with suspicion. He rolled over and looked me up and down.

'This is Major Lopta's personal plane, sir. Haven't you made a mistake?'

'Not as big a mistake as you are making interfering with me. How long has it been since you were a private?'

He looked at me in thought for a moment, then turned away without another word. I headed for the plane. As I climbed the ladder I saw that the noncom was busy at the radio in the car. This was a mistake on my part; I should have done something about that radio. As I was getting into the cockpit he dropped the radio and bellowed.

'Stop that man! He has no orders for this flight.'

The man steadying the ladder reached for my leg and I put my foot on his chest and pushed. I sent the ladder after him and dropped into the seat.

This situation had rapidly developed in a direction that was not to my liking. I had planned on having enough time to familiarize myself with the controls before I fired up the engines; although I had plenty of jet hours I had never been in a Cliaandian one before. Not only didn't I know where the starter was but I did some pretty desperate fumbling before I even found the switch for the instrument lights. As I flicked it on the ladder smacked back against the side of the plane. I hated old efficient noncoms, the backbone of the military. Now I had to take out time to open the flying suit and grope inside it for my pockets.

A few happy-gas and sleep grenades cleared away the mechanics for the moment. Some lay cheerfully unconscious while the others laughed themselves sick. The noncom had cowardly stayed out of range and was back on the radio again. I studied the instruments. There! The little black knob with PALJENJE on it. When I slapped it the jets whined and rumbled to life. A rocket slug crashed through the open canopy above my head and I ducked, cursing. As I kicked in the throttle I saw the noncom kneeling to take careful aim. The plane began to move – slowly.

His gun flared again and I felt the vibration as the slug buried itself in the seat. Which was probably armored. My first bit of luck. I flipped the tail so it pointed at the gunman, which put the armor between me and him and gave him a good blast of jet exhaust in the face. The plane bucked and shuddered and moved forward again – and I saw the torn fuel hose flapping in the windstream and pumping out its vital juices. Those idiots hadn't disconnected it! I didn't know where the fuel gauge was on the cluttered instrument board, nor did I want to look at it. Logic told me that gravity would bleed the fuel out a lot slower than the pumps had forced it into the tanks – but logic had nothing to do with this. I had a vision of the jets dying out here in the middle of the field while the forces of the enemy closed in around me. I could feel my blood pressure going up like an express elevator.

My busy little noncom friend was obviously still working on the radio, because when I turned onto the runway I saw that some trucks were moving into position to block it and something that looked suspiciously like an armored car was roaring up in the background. I cut the throttle back almost all the way and ducked my head down to read the instrument panel again.

What I was looking for wasn't there! Then I noticed another bank of switches on one side and painfully spelled out their messages in the bad light. ISBACIVANJE. There it was!

I looked up and saw that I was about to crash into the first truck. Men were baling out and running in all directions. My feet paddled about as I groped for the wheel brakes and I threw the rudder hard over. I finally found the brakes, stood on the right one and did a shuddering turn. About a half meter of wing tip tore off on the front of the truck. There was the orange blast of a gun as someone fired at me, but I have no idea where the

71

slug went. Then the jet was around and I was belting back in the opposite direction. This time at full throttle.

The runway lights were streaming by, faster and faster, and I had to keep one hand on the wheel while I groped for the belts and harnesses with the other. One of the buckles was missing and the end of the runway was coming up before I found out that I was sitting on it. I clicked it into place and grabbed the wheel with both hands as I ran out of runway.

The jet did not have flying speed. The nose was mushy and would not lift when I pulled back on it.

Then I was bumping across the graded dirt heading straight for that stone wall I had been looking at all evening.

Faster and faster to a certain collision.

CHAPTER NINE

THE TIMING had to be just right. Too early or too late would be just as disastrous. When the walls loomed up above the jet and I could see the joints between the blocks I figured it was about right and I hit the eject button.

Bam! The sequence was almost too fast to follow – but it worked. A transparent shutter snapped down over my face, the still tilted up canopy blew away with a crack of explosives, and the seat slammed up so hard against me that it felt like my spine had shortened to half its length. Almost in slow motion I sailed up and out of the jet and, for a hideously long second, saw the raw stone of the wall directly in front of me. Then I was over with only the dark sky ahead.

At the highest point in my arc there was another sharp crack at my back and I looked up to see the white column of the parachute swirling up above me. I was falling and the roofs of some buildings looked very close below.

The chute opened with a rustling snap, the seat pushed up against me and, a moment after this jarring deceleration, the wall of a building was rushing past and the seat hit the ground and rolled over. The chute settled slowly down and draped me in its enveloping folds.

I am chagrined to report that I did nothing at all at that moment. Events had moved even faster than I had planned and this final bit had been simply stunning. I gaped and gasped and shook my head and finally had enough sense to bang the quick release and throw off the harness straps.

After that I kept my head down and crawled and finally got out from under the chute.

A man and a woman had stopped on the opposite side of the street and were goggling in my direction. No one else was in sight. The only sign of activity seemed to be coming from the other side of the great black wall that loomed behind me. Flames lit the sky and smoke roiled and I could hear the loud popping of burning ammunition. Lovely.

'Testing new equipment,' I called out to the spectators and turned and trotted out of sight around the corner. In a dark doorway I stripped off the flying suit and dropped the helmet on top of it. Unidentified and free I strolled away towards the Robotnik. *Brilliantly conceived, Jim,* I told myself and gave myself a little pat on the shoulder.

At the same moment I realized that now that I was out of the base I would have to find a way to get back in before dawn, but I pushed this depressing revelation out of sight. First things first. I had to dispose of the real Vaska Hulja in order to take over his identity.

He was stirring when I came in, thrashing about in the bed and rocking his head back and forth. The hypnotic trance was wearing thin and he was fighting against it. Not that the robot cleaner was helping. It had dusted and cleaned the room and was now trying to make the bed with Vaska in it. I booted the thing in its COME BACK LATER button and ordered dinner for two. To take Vaska's subconscious mind off his troubles I gave him the strong suggestion that he had gone two days without eating and that this was the best meal he had ever had in his lifetime. He smacked and chortled and gurgled with delight while he ate; I just picked at my food. In the end I pushed it away and ordered Strong Drink in the hopes that the alcohol would stimulate or depress my thoughts into some coherent plan.

What was I to do with my companion here, happily

shoveling food into his gaping gob? His existence was a constant threat to my existence; there was room enough for only one Vaska Hulja in the scheme of things. Kill him? That would be easy enough. Dismember him in the bathtub and feed the parts and gallons of blood into an easily constructed arc furnace until I was left with a handful of dust. It was tempting, he had certainly killed enough people in his short and vicious lifetime to call this justice. But not tempting enough. Cold-blooded killing is just not my thing. I've killed in self-defense, I'll not deny that, but I still maintain an exaggerated respect for life in all forms. Now that we know that the only thing on the other side of the sky is more sky, the idea of an afterlife has finally been slid into the history books alongside the rest of the quaint and forgotten religions. With heaven and hell gone we are faced with the necessity of making a heaven or hell right here. What with societics and metatechnology and allied disciplines we have come a long way, and life on the civilized worlds is better than it ever was during the black days of superstition. But with the improving of here and now comes the stark realization that here and now is all we have. Each of us has only this one brief experience with the bright light of consciousness in that endless dark night of eternity and must make the most of it. Doing this means we must respect the existence of everyone else and the most criminal act imaginable is the terminating of one of these conscious existences. The Cliaandians did not think this way, which was why I intensely enjoyed dropping gravel in their gearboxes, but I still did. Which meant that I couldn't take the easy way out of reducing gravy-stained Vaska to his component molecules. If I did this I would be no better than they and I would be getting into the old game of the ends justifying the means and starting on that downward track.

I sighed, sipped, and the diagrams I had been visualizing for an arc furnace faded and vanished.

Well what then? I could chain him in a cave with an automatic food dispenser if I had a cave and so forth. Out. Given time and hard work I could alter his appearance and plant false memories that would last at least six months and get him into a prison or a work gang or a mental home or such. Except I did not have the time for anything this complex. I had until morning—or less— unless I wanted to abandon all the work I had already done in creating the false Vaska and having him accepted. They were probably getting involved in roll calls right now so I really should be thinking about ways of getting back into Glupost rather than worrying about my swinish companion. I noticed his stomach beginning to bulge so I turned off his appetite. He sat back and sighed and belched, with good reason. There was a rustling on the far wall as a panel slid back and the robot cleaner trundled in.

'May I give you a good cleaning?' it whispered in a sexy contralto voice. I told it what it could do, but it wasn't equipped to take this kind of instruction and only clicked and whirred until I ordered it to go to work. I watched it gloomily as it bustled about and made the bed—and the first spark of an idea began to glimmer in the darkness.

Vaska had stayed in the Robotnik for an entire day without any trouble. How long would it be possible to hold him here? Theoretically forever if enough money were deposited to the room's account. But he could not be kept subjugated by hypnosis for more than a day or two if I were not there to reinforce the suggestion. Or could he . . . ? I would have to find the control centre of the hotel before I could make any final decisions. But this could be the right idea.

I left Vaska watching an historic space opera on TV,

with the suggestion that this was the finest entertainment he had ever witnessed, which might possibly be the truth. Loaded with instruments and tools I went on the prowl. There would be a serviceway for the robots behind the rooms, but it was undoubtedly small, dark and dusty. That was a last resort. As mechanized as this hotel was, human beings had built it and could repair it if they had to. A quick prowl of the lower hallways near the entrance uncovered a concealed door with a disguised keyhole. It was flush with the wall and outlined with paneling, designed to be unobstrusive to maintain the fiction that the Robotnik was a hundred percent robot run. I spent more time with my instrumentation, making sure there were no bugs on the door, than I did opening it. The lock was a joke. There was no one in sight when I slipped through the door and closed it behind me.

I felt like a roach inside a radio. Electronic components hung, projected and bulged out on all sides; cables and wires looped and sagged in a profusion of electric spaghetti. Rolls of tape clicked and whirred on the computers, relays opened and closed, and gear trains chattered. It was a very busy place. I worked my way through it examining the labels and stepping over the little hutches where off duty robots rested, until I found what might be called a control centre. There was even a chair here before a console, that was designed for the human form, and I dropped into it. And set to work. I had been mulling my new plan over while tripping through this mechanical jungle and now knew what had to be done.

First, the electronic bugs in Vaska's room. I did not want him observed or listened to. The bugging circuits were easy enough to find and there was even a monitor screen that could be connected to any of them. I tested this out and apparently there was a bug in every room in the hotel and some interesting things were going on, but

77

I have never been much of a voyeur, preferring participation to observation, and a married man now as well. And time was passing quickly. All of the bugging circuits came together into a cable that vanished through the wall, to the local police station or other government bureau. Which gave me the idea. I had no time to fix a tape and soundtrack that would pump phoney information into the bugging circuit, I had to improvise. This was done easily enough by feeding the signal from the bugging circuit of another room into the wire from the room Vaska was occupying. From the way this setup was arranged it was obvious that the bugs were used to watch only one room at a time, for reasons best known to the people who built it. There was about one chance in ten thousand that it would ever be noticed that the same signal was coming from two rooms. And these odds were good enough for me. Over half of the rooms were empty in any case, which improved the odds even more.

Vaska could neither be seen nor heard now. The room and associated pleasures had to be paid for, but before I left I would deposit enough money (all stolen) to last a year if needs be.

A way to keep him in the room for that length of time was now needed and I – with my usual fertile imagination and basically nasty nature – had already devised that scheme. A small tape recorder was wired into the speaker circuit for the room, a timer attached, and the whole device concealed in the maze of other circuits and components. I programmed the tape, set the timer and started it up. Then rushed back to the room to watch my creation begin its job.

Vaska still had his eyes glued to the TV screen, panting with passion as mighty spaceships locked in frenzied destruction. Blasted cannon sizzled and ravening energies raved, and through this cut my recorded voice.

'Now hear this, Vaska, now hear this. You have had a long day and you are sleepy. You are yawning. You are going to turn off the lights and retire now, to sleep the sound sleep of the blessed for tomorrow is another day.'

And that was the big lie. For tomorrow would not be another day, not for dear Vaska. It was going to be the same one all over again. He would be lulled into a deep sleep and an even deeper trance by my soothing voice. And while there it would be explained to him that he would forget this day so he could wake up on the morning of his last day of leave before reporting for active duty. He would wake up with a slight hangover from the celebrations of the night before and would make an easy day of it. Just lie around the hotel room, read a bit, eat some food, watch TV, and retire early. He would enjoy himself. He would enjoy himself the same way every day until the programme was broken.

It was a wonderful plan and as foolproof as possible. I fed over half of my liquid funds into the paying hopper and the balance of the wall indicator shot up to an enormous number.

Slowly and happily, I reached out and hung the DO NOT DISTURB sign on the outside of the door.

And then I got depressed and turned the lights back on and looked around for the bottle that had provided me with so much inspiration so far. Vaska was well taken care of.

But how did I get back into the thrice-guarded and now doubly wakeful military base?

That high stone wall loomed as large in my brain as it did in reality. I had made a fuss going over it and alerted everyone. It would be nice if I could return without anyone knowing, sneaking under it perhaps. Out of the question, digging and earth moving and things like that could not be accomplished in a few hours. Steal a plane, fly over, parachute in? And be shot down before I hit the ground. There could be no worse time than the present to try to enter or leave the base. The guards would be suspicious and reinforced and the place crawling with troops. Which of course gave me the clue as to what I had to do. Turn their strength against them, use their own number to defeat them, judo on a giant basis. But how?

The answer came quickly enough once the problem had been correctly stated. I put together the equipment I would need, it was quite bulky, then stowed it all into a large suitcase and fitted the suitcase with a destruct apparatus. A disguise would be needed, nothing complex, just something to hide my real-assumed identity. Ahh, the levels of deception we must enter into. A long coat buttoned high concealed my uniform, my cap went into my pocket to be replaced by a floppy black hat, and my old faithful gray beard muzzled my face in anonymity. I was ready. I took a deep breath and a small drink and slipped out, locking the door behind me and pocketing the key. As I went out I slipped this into a waste chute and the flare of instant destruction brightened my way. Going a good distance from the hotel I signaled and a robocab stopped and I heaved in my suitcase.

'Main entrance, Glupost base,' I ordered and away we went.

Madness? Perhaps. But it was the only way.

Not that I didn't have a trapped butterfly or two beating for release from my stomach. This was only to be expected as we rolled up the approach street under the high lights, towards the suspicious and heavily armed guards who stood about fondling their weapons. Dawn was already lightening the sky.

'The base is closed!' a lieutenant shouted, pulling open the door of the cab. 'What are you doing here?'

'Base,' I quavered in a very bad imitation of an old

man's falsetto. 'Isn't this the Carrot Juice Centre for Natural Health? This cab has done me wrong . . . '

The officious lieutenant snorted through his nostrils and turned away – and I rolled a pair of gas grenades out through his bowed legs. And heaved five more after them. As the first ones went off I pulled the gas mask down out of my hat and slapped it over my face, beard and all.

My, but things got busy. The grenades were a fine mixture of blackout gas, smoke and happygas. Blind, laughing, cursing, coughing men stumbled about on all sides and a few guns went off. I worked my way through their confused ranks, sowing more confusion as I went, and up to the main gates and put down my suitcase and opened it. The shaped charges had adhesive bases and stuck to the steel of the gate when I slapped them into place.

A rocket slug burst against the gate and pieces of shrapnel tore at my flapping coat. I hit the ground. Tearing out two smoke grenades and dropping them behind me. Just as the smoke roiled up I had a quick glimpse of a squad coming up on the double, still outside the gassed area, firing as they came. Two more blackout gas bombs in that direction helped a lot. Now, as much in the dark as everyone else, I pushed in the caps by touch and linked them with fuse wire to the radio igniter.

Time was passing too quickly. They were alert inside the gate now and would be waiting for me. But I had come too far to back out. I closed the suitcase, again by touch, grabbed it up and inched my way along the wall and pressed the transmitter switch in my pocket.

Explosions banged out in the darkness and were followed by the clang of steel.

Hopefully an opening had been blasted in the gate.

I stumbled back towards it with all the sounds of bedlam in the darkness around me.

81

CHAPTER TEN

THE HOLE WAS THERE ALL RIGHT, with glimpses of lights on the other side as the smoke cloud roiled through it. There were troops there too because a hail of small arms fire clanged against the door with some chance slugs coming through the new-blasted opening. Screams sounded behind me as someone was hit. The fools were shooting each other, helping to spread the confusion I had sown. Keeping out of the line of fire from inside the gate I hurled grenade after grenade through and, when the smoke was at its thickest there, went through myself as fast and low as I could.

It really sounded great. Sirens were moaning, men shouting, weapons barking: the voices of utter confusion. I threw more grenades in all directions, throwing them as far as I could to widen the area of cover, until only a half dozen were left. These I saved for possible emergencies, which were sure to emerge, jamming them into my coat pockets. The self-destruct on the suitcase had a five second delay which I tripped, then hurled the suitcase away in the opposite direction. I crept along the wall, my only point of reference in the blackout, towards the guardhouse I had noticed when I had first examined the gate. There had been a clutch of vehicles parked there – at the time – and I muttered prayers that at least one of them still remained. The cloud thinned and I hurled two more grenades ahead of me. In the darkness I heard a motor start up.

Forgetting caution, I ran. Someone slammed into me

and fell heavily but I kept my feet and stumbled on. Then I tripped over a curb and did fall, but did a quick roll and came up running minus my hat. The engine was louder and then I saw the squarish van just beyond the edge of the smoke cloud. It was turning to start down the road and I threw two of my remaining four grenades as far ahead of it as I could. The driver hit the brakes as the mushrooming clouds sprang out, then I was at the door tearing it open. He was in cook's white, cap and all, and I reached out and dragged him to me, landing a swift right cross on his gaping jaw as he went by. Then I was in the driver's seat and pushing the thing into gear and jumping the deadweight of the vehicle forward as fast as I could, letting the door swing shut with the sudden acceleration. Once out of the smoke I saw that daylight had arrived.

Well done, I congratulated myself, then slowed down to avoid being conspicuous. More soldiers were coming down the street towards me, running at the double, so I slipped down as far as I could and began to tug at the gray beard. It was just about time to resume my Vaska identity.

A ringing pain possessed the side of my head and I fell over, shouting aloud at the sudden agony, pulling on the steering tiller as I went. The van rushed at the squad of soldiers who scattered in all directions. Something shiny flashed in the corner of my eye and I moved aside so the second blow caught me on the shoulder and was scarcely felt through all the clothing. A white clad arm holding a heavy pot projected in from the rear of the truck. I jammed the steering tiller hard over and the arm vanished from sight as its owner fell. In the rush I had forgotten there might be others in the van.

Just before the truck a frightened officer was spread-eagled against the wall. I pushed the tiller again and narrowly avoided him and we had a good look at each other as the van rushed by. He was sure to be impressed by my gasmask and beard and would instantly report it on his radio. Time was running out. Arm and pot reappeared and I chopped the wrist with the edge of my hand and gained possession of the pot. As soon as I had whipped the van around another corner, foot hard down on the throttle now, I threw the pot back to its owner with a blackout grenade inside, silencing at least this source of trouble for the moment. I straightened the weaving course of the van, gently touched the growing knot on my head, and noticed a brace of armored vehicles that appeared in the road ahead and turned in my direction. Buildings rushed by and I braked and turned into the next crossroad. The van was becoming more of a liability than an asset and I had to get rid of it.

But what then? I did not want to be found away from my quarters, this would bring instant suspicion, and the officers' buildings were in the opposite direction. But the officers' club was not too far away in the recreation area. Could I get there? Was it possible that the unconscious drunks of the previous evening's festivities still lay on the bunks where I had left them? This was too good a chance to miss, because if I could get back into my bunk I would certainly not be suspect.

This was close enough. There were vehicles coming towards me – and undoubtedly more behind me – but none close for the moment. I twisted the van into a narrow street, braked to a stop and hit the ground running. Shedding my disguise as I went, coat, beard, gas mask marking the trail behind me. I stuffed the remaining grenade into my pocket, pulled on my cap, squared my shoulders in a military manner, and strolled around the corner. A squad of soldiers were pouring out of barracks and forming ranks, but they ignored me, just another uniform among uniforms. The officers' club was not too far away. Two more corners and there it was. The front door sealed, but I knew the bunkroom entrance would be open.

Just as I was about to turn the corner I heard the men talking and I held back.

'Is that all?'

'Just a few more, sir, a couple that are hard to wake up. And one who won't get out of his bunk.'

'I'll talk to him.'

I took a quick look, then drew back.

I was too late. An officer was just entering the bunkroom door and plenty of soldiers were milling about, guiding hungover officers to a waiting truck. One of the officers was sitting on the ground, holding his head and ignoring the soldiers who were trying to entice him into the waiting transportation. Another was flipping his cookies against the wall of the building.

Think quickly, diGriz, time is running out. I bounced the last smoke grenade in my palm, then flipped the actuator with my thumb. If I could join the drunk team I would be safe; it would be worth the risk. I stepped around the corner, arm back, and no one was looking in my direction; with a quick heave I threw the grenade over the truck as far as it would go.

It exploded nicely, thud, boom, clouds of smoke and startled cries from the soldiery. And everyone looking in the same direction. Eight fast paces took me up behind them, to the seated officer who mumbled unhappily to himself, ignoring all else. I bent over, agreeing sympathetically with his half-heard complaints, helping him to his feet.

Then the soldiers were helping me, holding me as well since I seemed none too steady on my feet, guiding us both to the waiting truck. I tripped and almost fell and they caught and righted me. Now the stage was set – because there was one more thing I had to do. The cook in the truck would report that he had hit the spy on the head. So the word would be out to look for a head wound – like the one I had. I couldn't get rid of the knob on the side of my skull, but I could camouflage it. It would be painful, but it was necessary.

The soldiers helped me to the first step and I started up. As soon as they let go I missed the next step – and plummeted over backwards between them cracking my head on the ground.

I hit harder than I had planned and the blow on my already sore noggin felt like molten lead had been poured on it and I must have passed out for a moment. When I recovered I was sitting up with blood running down the side of my face – I hadn't planned that but it certainly made a nice touch – and a soldier was running up with a first aid kit. I was bandaged and calmed and this time helped all the way into the truck: I felt awful which was fine. With dragging feet I groped my way to the far end, as far from the entrance as I could get, where a voice called out hollowly to me.

'Vaska . . . ' It changed to a hollow coughing.

My room mate Ostrov was there, looking rumpled and miserable.

'You don't have a drink?' he asked, his usual morning salutation.

I gave him sympathy, if not beverage, during our brief ride.

There were aggrieved cries when the wheeled drunk tank was unloaded and the officers saw that they had not been returned to their quarters, but had been brought instead to one of the administration buildings. I complained along with the others, although I had been expecting something like this. Someone had escaped from the Glupost base, someone else had entered. Every head would have to be counted until the missing and/or extra party could be found. We were guided, stumbling, into a waiting area, to be called out one by one to confer with a battery of tired clerks. While we waited there was a brisk amount of business back and forth to the latrine and I joined the queue. Mainly to leave a little soap on my fingers when I washed my hands, so I could rub some of it into my eyes. It burned like acid, but I let it stay for a moment before I rinsed it out. My eyes glared back at me from the mirror like twin coals of fire. Perfect.

On cue, I found the clerk, showed my identification and had my name checked off on a roster. I hoped, like all the others, that we would be allowed to leave soon. Many of them had gone to sleep on the benches and I joined their number. It had been a strenuous night. What better disguise for the spy than sleeping in the heart of the enemy?

It was the sudden silence that shook me awake. I had been lulled off by the grumbles and complaints of my fellow officers, the coming and going of soldiers, the busy whir of office machines. These noises had all stopped, and had been replaced by silence. Through the silence, first distant, then louder and louder came the sound of a single set of footsteps approaching slowly and steadily. They came towards me – and passed by, and I kept my eyes closed and forced myself to breathe regularly. Only when they were well past did I open my eyes a crack.

I wondered at the silence. All I saw was the back of the man, a nondescript back slightly bent, a wrinkled uniform of unimpressive pale gray and a cap of the same fabric. I could not recall seeing this particular uniform before. I wondered what the fuss was about. Yawning, I sat up and scratched my head below the bandage, watching as the man reached the end of the room and turned to face us all. He was no more prepossessing from the front than from the back. Sandy hair getting a little thin on top, an incipient roll of fat and double chin, clean shaven with an unmemorable face. Yet when he spoke, in the tones of a stern schoolmaster, all of the veteran officers present remained dead silent.

'You officers, the few among you who were sober enough that is, may have heard an explosion and seen a cloud of smoke while you were on the way here. This explosion was caused by an individual who entered this base and is still undetected in our midst. We know nothing about him, but suspect that he is an offworld spy . . .'

This drew a gasp and a murmer as might be expected and the gray man waited a moment until he continued.

'We are making an intensive search for this individual. Since you gentlemen were in the immediate vicinity I am going to talk to you one at a time to find out what you might know. I also may discover . . . which one of you is the missing spy.'

This last shaft exacted only a shocked silence. Now that he had everyone in the mental condition for cross-examining the gray man began calling officers forward one at a time. I was doubly grateful for the foresight that had dropped me off the truck onto the side of my head.

It was no accident that I was the third man called forward. On what grounds? General resemblance in build to the offworld spy Pas Ratunkowy? My delayed arrival at Glupost? The bandage? Some basis of suspicion must have existed. I dragged forward with slow speed just as the others had done. I saluted and he pointed to the chair next to the desk.

'Why don't you hold this while we talk,' he said in a reasonable voice, passing over the silver egg of a polygraph transmitter.

The real Vaska would not have recognized it, so I didn't. I just looked at it with slight interest – as though I did not know it was transmitting vital information to the lie detector before him – and clutched it in my hand. My thoughts were not as calm.

I'm caught! He has me! He knows who I am and is just toying with me!

He looked deep into my bloodshot eyes and I detected a slight curl of distaste to his mouth.

'You have had quite a night of it, Lieutenant Hulja,' he said quietly, his eyes on the sheaf of paper – and on the lie detector readout as well.

'Yes sir, you know . . . having a few last drinks with the boys.' That was what I said aloud. What I thought was *They will shoot me, dead, right through the heart!* and I could visualize that vital organ spouting my life's blood into the dirt.

'I see you recently had your rank reduced – and where are your fuses, Pas Ratunkowy?'

Am I tired . . . wish I was in the sack I thought.

'Fuses, sir?' I blinked my red orbs and reached to scratch my head and touched the bandage and thought better of it. His eyes glared into mine, gray eyes almost the color of his uniform, and for a moment I caught the strength and anger behind his quiet manners.

'And your head wound – where did you get that? Our offworld spy was struck on the side of the head.'

'I fell, sir, someone must have pushed me. Out of the truck. The soldiers bandaged it, ask them . . . '

'I already have. Drunk and falling down and a disgrace to the officer corps. Get away and clean yourself up, you disgust me. Next man.'

I climbed unsteadily to my feet, not looking into the steady glare of those cold eyes, and started off as though I had forgotten the device in my hand, then turned back and dropped it on his desk, but he was bent over the papers and ignoring me. I could see a faint scar under the thin hair of his balding crown. I left.

Fooling a polygraph takes skill, practice and training. All of which I had. It can only be done in certain circumstances and this one had been ideal. A sudden interview without normalizing tests being run on the subject. Therefore I began the interview in a near panic – before any questions had been asked. All of this must have peaked nicely on his graph. I was afraid. Of him, of something, anything. But when he had asked the loaded questions meant to uncover a spy – the question I knew was coming – I had relaxed and the readout had shown this. The question was a meaningless one to anyone but the offworlder. Once he saw this the interview was over, he had plenty more to do.

Ostrov was sitting up, cold sober, eyes as big as plates when I came back and dropped onto the bench next to him.

'What did he want?' He spoke in a hollow whisper.

'I don't know. He asked me something or other that I didn't know about and then it was over.'

'I hope he doesn't want to talk to me.'

'Who is he?'

'Don't you *know!*' with shocked incredulity. I tread warily, covering my complete lack of information.

'Well you know I just came here . . . '

'But *everyone* knows Kraj.'

'Is that *him* . . . ?' I gasped it out and tried to look as frightened as he did and it semed to work, because he nodded and looked over his shoulder and quickly back again. I rose and went to the latrine again to terminate the conversation at this spot. Everyone knew about Kraj.

Who was Kraj?

CHAPTER ELEVEN

EMBARKING FOR THE INVASION came as a relief for everyone; better a nice quiet war than the suspicions and fears that swept the Glupost base during the following days. There were sudden inspections, midnight searches, constant alarms and the sound of marching boots at all hours. I would have been proud of my efforts at sowing the seeds of disorder if I had not been a victim of that disorder at the same time. The invasion plans must have gone ahead too far to alter because, in the midst of all the excitement, we still adhered to schedule. On B day minus two all the bars closed so that the sobering up process of the troops could begin. A few reluctant ones, myself and Ostrov included, had concealed bottles which carried us a bit further, but even this ended when our lockers and bags were put into storage and we were issued pre-packed invasion kits. I had a small can of powdered alcohol disguised as tooth powder that I was saving for an emergency and the emergency instantly presented itself as the thought of the coming weeks without drink, so Ostrov and I finished the tooth powder on B Day minus one and that was that. After one last midnight spot check and search we were assembled and marched to the departure area. The fleet, row after row of dark projectiles, stood waiting beyond the gates. We were called out, one at a time, and sent to our assigned places.

In the beginning I had thought that this was a rather stupid way to run an invasion. No plans, no diagrams, no peptalk, no training, no maneuvers – no nothing. It finally dawned on me that this was the ideal way to mount an invasion that you wished to keep secret. The pilots had plenty of piloting experience, and we would get more on the outward voyage. The troops were ready to fight; the sources of supply supplied. And somewhere at the top there were locked boxes of plans, course tapes and such. None of which would be opened until we were safe in warpdrive and outside communication would be impossible. All of which made life easier for me since there were few opportunities to trip me up in my knowledge of things Cliaandian.

It was with a great deal of pleasure that I found myself assigned as pilot of a troop transport. This was a role I could fill with honor. My earlier assignment of a room mate had not been accidental either, because Ostrov climbed into the navroom a few minutes later and announced that he was going to be my copilot.

'Wonderful,' I told him. 'How many hours do you have on one of these Pavijan class transports?'

He admitted to an unhappily low figure and I patted him on the shoulder.

'You are in luck. Unlike most First Pilots your old Uncle Vaska is without ego. For an old drinking buddy no sacrifice is too great. I am going to let you fire the takeoff and if you do the kind of job I think you will do, then I might let you shoot the landing as well. Now hand me the check list.'

His gratitude was overwhelming, so much so that he admitted that he had been saving his fountain pen for a real emergency since it was filled with 200 proof alcohol and we both had a squirt. It was with a feeling of content-ment – and scarred throats – that we watched the troops marching up and filing into the loading ports far below. A few minutes later a grizzled fullbearded colonel in combat uniform stamped into the navroom.

'No passengers allowed here,' I said.

'Shut your mouth, lieutenant. I have your course tapes.'

'Well, let me have them?'

'What? You must be either mad or joking – and both are shooting offenses in combat.'

'I must be on edge, colonel, not much sleep, you know . . .'

'Yes.' He relented slightly. 'Allowances must be made, I suppose. It hasn't been easy for anyone. But that's behind us now. Victory for Cliaand!'

'Victory for Cliaand!' we entolled ritually. There had been a lot of this the last couple of days. The Colonel looked at his watch.

'Almost time. Get the command circuit,' he ordered.

I pointed to Ostrov, who pressed the right button instantly. A message appeared on the comscreen. STAND BY. We stood. Then it began blinking quickly and changed to the harsh letters, SET COURSE. The colonel took the tape container from his pouch and we had to sign as witnesses on a form stating that the tape was sealed when we received it. Ostrov inserted the tape into the computer and the colonel grunted in satisfaction, his work done, and turned to leave. He fired a parting shot over his shoulder on the way out.

'And none of those 10 G landings that you moronic pilots seem to enjoy. I'll courtmartial you both if that happens.'

'Your mother knits sweaters out of garbage,' I shouted after him, waiting, of course, until the door was closed. But even this feeble effort stirred enthuiasm in Ostrov who was beginning to respect me more and more.

Hurry up and wait is common to all military forces and that is what we did next. The check lists were complete and we saw ship after ship take off until most were gone. The transports were last. The green BLASTOFF signal came as a relief. We were on our way. To a nameless planet circling an unknown star as far as any of us were concerned. The tape told the computer where we were going but did not condescend, nor had it been programmed, to inform us.

This security blanket lasted right up to the invasion itself. We were seven boring days en route with nothing to drink and the ship piloted by the computer and the frozen rations barely edible. On a long term basis, without the ameliorating effects of alcohol, Ostrov proved to be less than a sparkling companion. No matter where the conversation began it invariably ended up in repetitive anecdotes from his school days. I slept well, I'll say that, and usually while he was talking but he never seemed to mind. I also checked him out on the instruments with drills and dry runs, which may have done him some active good and certainly acquainted me with the controls and operation of the ship.

Since the ship was completely automated, Ostrov and I were the only crew members aboard. The single doorway to the troop area was sealed and my friend the surly colonel had the only key. He visited us once or twice which was no pleasure at all. On the seventh day he was standing behind us glowering at the back of my neck when we broke out of warpdrive and back into normal space.

'Take this, inspect here, sign that,' he snapped and we did all those things before he broke the seal on the flat case. This was labeled INVASION in large red letters which rather suggested that things would be hotting up soon. My instructions were simple enough and I switched on the circuits as ordered so the ship could home on the squadron leader. A yellowish sun shone brightly off to one side and the blue sphere of a planet was on the other. The colonel glared at this planet as though he wanted to reach out and grab it and take a bite out of it, so future developments seemed obvious enough without asking questions.

The invasion began. Most of the fleet was ahead of us, lost in the night of space and visible only occasionally as a network of sparks when they changed course. Our squadron of transports stayed together, automatically following the course set by the lead ship, and the planet grew in the screens ahead. It looked peaceful enough from this distance, though I knew the advance units of the fleet must be attacking by this time.

I was not looking forward to this invasion – who but a madman can enjoy the prospect of approaching war? – but I was hoping to find out the answer to the question that had brought me here. I believed that interplanetary invasions were *still* impossible, despite the fact that I was now involved in one myself. I felt somewhat like the man who, upon seeing one of the most exotic animals in the zoo, said 'there ain't no such animal'. Interplanetary invasion just don't work.

The interplanetary invading force rushed on, a mighty armada giving the lie to my theories. As the nameless planet grew larger and larger, filling the forward screens, I could see the first signs of the war that I knew was already in progress; tiny sparkles of light in the night hemisphere. Ostrov saw them too and waved his fist and cheered.

'Give it to them, boys,' he shouted.

'Shut up and watch your instruments,' I snarled. Suddenly hating him. And instantly relenting. He was a product of his environment. As the twig is bent so grows the bough and so forth. His twig had been bent nicely by the military boarding school into which he had been stuffed as a small child. Which, for some unknown reason, he still thought well of although every story he told me about it had some depressing or sadistic point to make. He had been raised never to question, to believe God had created Cliaand a bit better than all the other planets, and that they were therefore ordained to take care of the inferior races.

It is amazing the things people will believe if you catch them early enough.

Then we were turned loose as the individual transports scattered to home in on their separate targets. I fiddled with the radio and silently cursed the Cliaandian passion for security and secrecy. Here I was landing a shipload of troops – and I didn't even know where! On the planet below, surely, they could not very well disguise that fact, but on what continent? At what city? All I knew was that pathfinder ships had gone in first and planted radio beacons. I had the frequency and the signal I was to listen for, and when I detected it I was to home in and land. And I knew that the target was a spaceport. With the final instructions I had received some large and clear photographs – the Cliaandian spies had obviously been hard at work – of a spaceport; aerial and ground views. A big red X was marked near the terminal buildings and I had to set the ship as close to this site as I could. Fine.

'That's the signal!' The dah-dah-dit-dah was loud and clear.

'Strap in – here we go,' I said, and fed instructions to the computer. It worked up landing orbit almost instantly and the main jets fired. 'Give the colonel the first warning, then feed him proximity and altitude reports while I bring her in.'

We were dropping towards the terminator, flying into the dawn. The computer had a fix on the transmitter and was bringing us down in a slow careful arc. When we broke through the cloud cover and the ground was visible far below I saw the first sign of any resistance. The black clouds of explosions springing up around us.

'They're shooting at us,' Ostrov gasped, shocked.

'Well, it's a shooting war, isn't it?' I wondered what kind of veteran he was to be put off by a little gunfire, and at the same time I hit the computer override and turned off the main jets. We dropped into free fall and the next explosions appeared above and behind us as the gun computer was thrown off by our deceleration change.

I caught sight of the spaceport below and hit the lateral jets to move us in that direction. But we were still falling. Our radar altimeter readings were being fed into the computer which kept flashing red warnings about the growing proximity of the ground. I gave it a quick program to hold landing deceleration as long as possible, to drop us at 10 G's to zero altitude. This meant we would be falling at maximum speed and slowing down for minimum time, which would decrease the time we would be exposed to ground fire. And I wanted the colonel to have the 10 G's he had once warned me about.

The jets fired at what looked like treetop height, slamming us down into our couches. I smiled, which is hard to do with ten gravities pulling at you, thinking about the expression on the colonel's face at that moment. Watching the screen I added some lateral drift until we were just over the hardstand which was our target area. After this it was up to the computer which did just fine and killed the engines just as our landing struts crunched down. As soon as all the engines cut off I hit the disembark button and the ship shivered as the ramps blew out and down.

'That takes care of our part,' I said, unbuckling and stretching.

Ostrov joined me at the viewport as we watched the troops rush down the ramps and run for cover. They did not seem to be taking any casualties at all which was surprising. There were some bomb craters visible nearby and heaps of rubble, while fighter-bombers still roared low giving cover. But it didn't seem possible that all resistance had been knocked out this quickly. Unless this world did not have much of a standing army. That might be one answer to explain the Cliaandian invasion success; only pick planets that are ripe for plucking. I made a mental note to look into this. Well behind his troops came the colonel in his command car. I hoped that his guts were still compressed from the landing.

'Now we have to find some drink,' Ostrov said, smacking his lips in anticipation.

'I'll go,' I said, taking my sidearm from the rack and buckling it on. 'You stay with the radio and watch the ship.'

'That's what all the first pilots always say,' he complained, so I knew I had called this one right.

'Privilege of rank. Someday you will be exercising it too. I shouldn't be long.'

'Spaceport bar, that's where it usually is,' he called after me.

'Don't teach your grandpa to chew cheese,' I sneered, having already figured that one out.

All of the interior doors had unlocked automatically when we landed. I climbed the ladders down to the recently vacated combat deck and kicked my way through the discarded ration containers to the nearest ramp. The fresh sweet air of morning blew in, carrying with it the smell of dust and explosives. We had brought the benefits of Cliaandian culture to another planet.

I could hear firing in the distance and a jet thundered by and was gone, but after this it was very quiet. The invasion had fanned out from the spaceport leaving a pocket of silence in its wake. Nor was anyone in sight when I walked, unexamined, through the customs area and, with reflex skill, found the bar. The first thing I did was to drain a flask of beer, then poured a small Antarean *ladevandet* to hold it down. There were ranked bottles behind the bar, new friends and old ones, and I made a good selection. I needed something to carry them in and opened one of the sliding doors beneath, looking for a box or a bag, and found myself staring into the frightened eyes of a young man.

'*Ne mortigu min!*' he cried. I speak Esperanto like a native and answered him in the same tongue.

'We are here to liberate you so mean you no harm.' Word of this conversation might get to the authorities and I wanted to make the right impression. 'What is your name?'

'Pire.'

'And the name of this world?' This seemed sort of a dim question for an arrogant invader to ask, but he was too frightened to question it.

'Burada.'

'That's fine, I'm glad you decided to be truthful. And what can you tell me about Burada?'

Badly phrased, admittedly, and he was too stunned to answer. He gaped for a moment, then climbed out of the cabinet and turned to root about in it. He came up with a booklet that he passed over in silence. It had a 3D cover of an ocean with graceful trees on the bordering shore, that sprang to life as soon as the heat of my hand touched it; the waves crashed silently on the golden sands and the trees moved to the touch of unfelt breezes. Letters formed of clouds moved across the sky and I read BEAUTIFUL BURADA . . . HOLIDAY WORLD OF THE WESTERN WARP . . .

'Looting and consorting with the enemy,' a familiar, and detested, voice said from the doorway. I turned slowly to see my friend the colonel from our ship standing there fingering his gaussrifle with what can only be termed a filthy grin on his face.

'And 10 G landing too,' he added, undoubtedly the real cause of his unhappiness. 'Which is not a shooting offense although the other two are.'

CHAPTER TWELVE

PIRE SHRIEKED IN A MUFFLED MANNER and drew back, not understanding the colonel's words but recognizing his manner and his weapon. I smiled, as coldly as I could, as I saw that my hands were out of sight below the bar. Turning to the youth I pointed to the far end of the room and ordered him there. He scuttled nicely and while this bit of mis-direction was going on I slipped the tourist book into my pocket and eased my gausspistol out of its holster. When I turned back to the colonel I saw that he had half raised his rifle.

'You are wrong,' I said, 'and insulting as well to a fellow officer who recently was a flight-major. I am aiding our invading forces by securing this drinking establishment to prevent any of *your* troops from becoming drunk on duty and therefore injuring our all-out efforts. And while in this place I took a prisoner who was hiding here. That is what happened and it is my word against yours, colonel.'

He raised his gun barrel towards me and said, 'It is only my word that I caught you looting and was forced to shoot you when you resisted arrest.'

'I am a hard one to shoot,' I said, letting the muzzle of my pistol slide up over the edge of the bar until it was centered between his eyes. 'I am an expert shot and one of these explosive slugs will take the top of your head off.'

Apparently he had not expected this kind of instant response from a flying officer and he hesitated for a moment. Pire squealed faintly and there was a thud. I assumed he had fainted but was too busy to look. This murderous tableau held for a moment and there was no way of knowing how it might have ended if a soldier had not rushed into view with a field radio. The colonel took the phone and went back to the war while I stuffed two bottles into the back of my jacket and went out the other exit, stepping over Pire who was unconscious on the floor and undoubtedly better off that way. I was gone before the colonel realized it and I took the drink back to the ship and sent it up the service lift to Ostrov. 'And don't drink more than one,' I ordered and his voice responded with a happy cry over the intercom.

I was on my own now and I meant to make the most of my opportunity. With the battle still being waged my movements would not be watched and I could make my observations. Of course I might also be killed, but that is one of the occupational hazards of the service. Once the invasion had succeeded movement would be sharply restricted and I would probably be on my way back to Cliaand. The guide booklet was still in my pocket, the heat of my hip keeping the action going on the cover. I opened it and flipped through the pages which were heavy on pictures and short on copy. This was the hard sell all right with low music coming from the illustration of the floating orchestra on beautiful Sabun Bay and the scent of flowers from the Kanape fields. I expected some snow to fall out of the picture of skiing in the Kar mountains, but the technology of advertising did not extend this far. There was a map showing the airport and the city, diagrammatic and worthless for the most part, though it did tell me I was standing in Sucuk Spaceport close by Sucuk City. I threw away the book and went to see the sights.

Depressing. It would be a long time before the tourists came back to these sunny shores. I walked through the empty streets, pocked by explosions and charred by fire, and wondered what the purpose of this could possibly be.

War, always a foolish business, seemed even more infantile at this moment. Horrible might be a better word; I saw my first corpses. There was the sound of dragging feet and a horde of prisoners appeared in the street ahead, guarded on all sides by alert Cliaandian troops. Many of the prisoners were wounded and few bandaged. The sergeant in charged saluted when they went by and gave a wave of victory. I smiled in return but it took an effort. What I had to do now was to find some responsible citizen of Sucuk City who was not yet a prisoner or dead and get the answers to some questions.

The citizen found me first. I left the main road and turned down a narrow winding street ominously labeled Matbaacilik-sasurtmek – any street with a name like that could not be all good. My suspicions had some justification in fact. I discovered this when I turned a sharp corner and found myself facing a young woman who was pointing a large bore hunting rifle at me. I was waving my little fingers in the air even before she spoke.

'Surrender or die!'

'I've surrendered – can't you see! Long live Burada, rah-rah . . .'

'None of your sickening jokes, you foul war-mongering male, or I'll shoot you on the spot.'

'I'm on your side, believe me. Peace on Burada, good will to men – and women too of course.'

She snorted at this and waved me towards a dark doorway with the gun. Even in anger she was a handsome woman, wide-faced with flaring nostrils and black hair hanging straight to her shoulders. She wore a dark green uniform, high boots, leather straps and all, with some kind of insignia on the sleeve. She was feminine despite this; no uniform could be made to disguise the magnificent swell of that bosom. I entered the doorway as she demanded and she reached to take my pistol as I passed.

I could have done some quick business then with her arm
and the gun barrel and ended up with both weapons, but I
restrained myself. As long as she felt she was in charge she
might talk more easily. We entered a dark inner room with
a single window, an office of some kind, where another girl
in uniform was stretched out on the desk. Her eyes were
closed and the leg of her uniform had been cut away to
disclose an ugly wound now bound with clumsy bandages.
Blood had seeped through them and pooled upon the
desk top.

'You have medicine?' my captress asked.

'I do,' I said, opening the medpack at my waist. 'But I
don't think it will do much good. She appears to have lost
a lot of blood and needs medical attention.'

'Where will she get it? Not from you swine invaders.'

'Perhaps.' I was busy with pressure points, tearing off the
old bandages, sprinkling on antiseptic powder and apply-
ing better bandages. 'Her pulse is slow and very weak. I
don't think she will make it.'

'If she doesn't – you killed her.' Tears were in my
opponent's eyes, though this did not stop her from keeping
the blunderbuss pointed at my midriff.

'I'm trying to save her, remember? And you can call me
Vaska.'

'Taze,' she said automatically. 'Sergeant in the Guard
before *they* took over.'

'They?' I felt slightly confused. 'You mean them, *us*, the
army of Cliaand?'

'No, of course not. But why am I talking to you when I
should be killing you . . .'

'You shouldn't. Kill me, I mean. Would you believe me
if I told you I was a friend?'

'No.'

'That I was a spy from elsewhere now working against
the Cliaands although I am in their Space Armada?'

'I would say that you are a worm pleading for your worthless life and willing to say anything.'

'Well, it's true, anyway,' I grumbled, realizing she wasn't going to take my revelations on faith.

'Taze . . .' the girl on the table said weakly and we both turned that way. Then 'Taze' again and died.

I thought I was dead as well. Taze swung the rifle up and I could see her knuckles whiten as she squeezed. I did a lot of things quickly, starting with a dive to get under the gun and a roll right into her. The gun fired – the blast almost taking my head off in the confined space – but I wasn't hit. Before she could fire again I had the barrel in my hand and did a quick chop at the muscles in her arm and a few other things one does not normally do to women except in an emergency like this. Then I had the rifle, as well as my pistol back, and she was lying against the wall with something to really cry about this time. It would be a number of minutes before she could use her fingers again; I had stopped just short of breaking the bone.

'Look, I'm sorry,' I said, putting my pistol away and fumbling with the archaic mechanism of the rifle. 'I just didn't feel like getting killed at the moment and this was the only way I could stop you.' I worked the bolt and ejected all the cartridges, then squinted inside to make sure I hadn't missed any. 'What I told you was true. I am on your side and want to help you. But you will have to help me first.'

She was puzzled, but I had her attention. She wiped her eyes on her sleeve when I handed back her rifle, then widened them when I passed over the ammunition.

'I would appreciate it if you would keep that weapon unloaded for the moment. I'll trade you information if you don't want to give it freely. There is an organization you probably never heard of who is very interested in what the Cliaand are doing. And what they are doing is interstellar invasion – Burada is the sixth on the list and it looks as though it will be as successful as the others.'

'But why do they do this?'

I had her interest now and I rushed on.

'The why isn't important, at least not for the present, since evil ambitions are not unusual among the varied political forms of mankind. What I want to know is the *how*. How did they get away with this invasion in the face of the defences of the planet?'

'Blame the Konsolosluk,' she said with vehemence, shaking the rifle. 'I'm not saying that the Women's Party didn't make mistakes, but nothing like theirs.'

'Could you fill in some background detail, because I'm afraid you've lost me.'

'I'll give you detail. Men!' She spat and her eyes glowed with anger and she was beginning to look attractive again. 'The Women's Party brought centuries of enlightened rule to this planet. We had prosperity, there was a good tourist trade, no one suffered. So maybe men voted a few years later than women or couldn't get the best jobs. So what? Women suffered through this sort of thing – and worse – on other planets, and they didn't revolt. Those Konsolosluk, sneaking around everywhere, whispering lies. Men's rights and down with oppression and that kind of thing. Getting people worked up, winning a few seats in parliament, disturbing the country. Then their one day revolution, seizing everything, getting control. And all their promises. All they wanted to do was strut around and act superior. Some superior! Worthless, all of them. Know nothing of Government or fighting. When your pigs landed more of these *men* ran away than fought, weak fools. And surrendering rather than fighting. I would never have surrendered.'

'Perhaps they had to.'

'Never. Weaklings, that's all.'

All of which gave me pause to think, and with thought

came suspicion and after this the dawning light of discovery. Pieces began to fall into shape in my mind and I tried not to get too excited. It was a formless idea yet – but if it worked – if it worked!

Then I would know how the Cliaandians managed their invasion trick. Simple, like all good ideas, and foolproof as well.

'I'll need your help,' I told Taze. 'I'll stay in the Space Armada, at least for the moment, since I can learn more there. But I won't leave this planet. This is where the Cliaandians are the weakest and this is where they are going to be beaten. Have you ever heard of the Special Corps?'

'No.'

'Well, you have now. It is, well, it is the group that is going to help you. I work for them and they should be keeping an eye on me. They saw the fleet leave Cliaand and are certain to have followed it here. That was one of the developments we had planned for. Right now a message drone should be circling this planet. It will relay any messages to the Corps and we will have all the help we need. Can you get access to a medium powered radio transmitter?'

'Yes – but why should I? Why should I believe you? You could be lying.'

'I could be – but you can't take the chance.' I scratched feverishly on a message form. 'I'm leaving you now, I have to get back to my ship before they begin to wonder where I have gone. Here is the message you are to transmit on this frequency. You can do it without getting caught, it's easy enough. And you lose nothing by doing it. And you may save your planet.'

She was still doubtful, looking at the paper.

'It's so hard to believe. That you really are a spy – and want to help us.'

'You can believe he is a spy, take my word for it,' a voice said from the doorway behind me and I felt a cold hand clamp down on my heart. I turned, slowly.

Kraj, the man in gray, was standing there. Two other gray uniformed men stood behind him leveling their weapons at me. Kraj pointed his finger like a third gun.

'We have been watching you, spy, and waiting for this information. Now we can proceed with the destruction of your Special Corps.'

CHAPTER THIRTEEN

'PEOPLE SEEM TO BE POPPING up in doorways a lot today, ha ha,' I said with a joviality I certainly did not feel. Kraj smiled a very wintry smile.

'If you mean the colonel, yes, I had him watching you. Now try to act the fool, Pas Ratunkowy, or whatever your name really is.'

'Hulja, Vaska, Lieutenant in the Space Armada.'

'Flight-Major Hulja has been found in the Dosadan-Glup Robotnik Hotel, which discovery put us on your trail. Yours was a most ingenious plan and might have succeeded had not an optical pickup burned out. The repairman sent to order the matter discovered the Flight-Major and his delusion about the date and this was brought to my attention. I'll take that.'

Kraj lifted the message form from Taze's unresisting fingers. He seemed very much in control of the situation. I clutched my chest in the area of my heart, rolled up my eyes and staggered backwards.

'Too much . . .' I muttered. 'Heart going . . . don't shoot . . . this is the end.'

Kraj and his two men looked on coldly while I was going through all this for their benefit, until the dramatic moment when I clutched at my throat and shrieked with pain, my body arched and every muscle taut, then fell backwards through the window.

It was done with plenty of crashing glass, and I flipped in midair and landed on my shoulder and did a roll and came up on my feet, ready to run.

Looking right up the barrel of a gaussrifle held by another silent and unsmiling man in gray. He scored zero as a conversationalist and for the moment I could think of nothing bright to say myself. Kraj's voice came clearly through the broken window behind me.

'Take the girl to the prison camp, we have no further need for her. The rest of us will return with the spy. Be on guard constantly, you have seen what he can do.'

Not very much, I thought to myself in a sudden gloomy depression. Not very much at all. I had penetrated all right, and found out what I wanted to know, but I had not been able to get my information out. Which made it useless. Worse than useless. Kraj might be able to turn my message to his own ends which I was sure were pretty nasty ones. This dark state of mind persisted while the rest of the doom-faced gray men surrounded me and trotted me off to a waiting truck. There was no chance at all to escape; they were very efficient with those guns.

It was a brief trip, though a remarkably uncomfortable one. The vehicle was a captured Burada truck that must have been used for the transport of garbage or something worse. I was the only one who seemed bothered by the permeating smell. The gray neither commented on it nor took their eyes from me once during the trip. At least the vehicle was silent and smooth; it burned gas in a fuel cell to generate electricity – supplied to a separate drive motor in each wheel. I considered desperate plans of ripping up one of the cables where it passed by my feet, or leaping out of the rear of the truck and so forth. None of this was much good and we reached our destination with our relative positions unchanged. At gunpoint I was herded into a commandeered building, into an empty room where, still at gunpoint, I was ordered to strip. With a portable fluoroscope and cold probes, most humiliating, they removed all devices and gadgetry from my person, then gave me new clothes.

These clothes were something else again. A single-piece overall made of soft and flexible plastic, they provided protection and warmth for the wearer. Yet they were ideal prison dress because they were completely transparent. This continual shielded-nakedness was certainly not morale building and I began to have even more respect for the gray men. And everything done in silence despite my attempts at conversation. The final sartorial touch was a metal collar that locked around my neck. A cable ran from the collar to a box one of the gray men held. All of this had a very ominous look to it. My suspicions were justified when the others left with all of the weapons and he faced me, box in hand.

'I can do this,' he said in a voice as gray as his garb and pressed a button on the box.

The thing I experienced next was quite unexpected and singularly painful. In a single instant I was blinded by exploding lights of a color and fury I had never seen before. Sound greater than sound filled my ears and every square inch of my skin burned with a fire as though I had been dropped into an acid bath. These interesting things went on for a longer time than I really appreciated and then suddenly vanished as quickly as they had begun. Sight and hearing returned and I found myself lying on the floor with a sore spot on the back of my head where I had cracked it when I fell. It felt rather good just to lie there. That little box must generate neural currents on selected frequencies. No need to torture the body when you can feed specific pain impulses into the nervous system.

'Stand,' my captor said, and I did rather quickly.

'If you wish to convey the message that you can do that whenever you want, and right now you want me to behave – the message has been received. But speak and I shall obey. I'll be a good boy.'

For the time being. Until I found a way to get out of this stainless steel rat trap. I trotted along docilely to another room where Kraj waited for me behind a large metal desk. The room was dusty and blank areas on the wall showed where pictures and pieces of furniture had been removed. The only new item, other than the desk, was a shining hook recently affixed in the ceiling. I was not at all surprised when the hook fitted into a ring on the box and I was leashed, standing before my captor.

Kraj looked me up and down, examining me closely, a very easy thing to do considering the transparent condition of my clothing. I have never suffered from a nudity taboo so this did not bother me. It was the cold and unemotional look in his eyes that was more offputting. At the present moment I was, to use the classical term, completely at his mercy. I had no idea of what nastiness he had in mind for me and I determined to at least attempt to ameliorate it a bit.

'What would you like to know?' I asked.

'A number of things, but that will come later.'

'What's wrong with now? Considering the state of modern hypnotic techniques, drug therapy and old-fashioned torture – like your nerve machine here – it is impossible to keep facts from a determined interrogator. Therefore ask and I shall answer.' What little I knew about the Special Corps he was welcome to. All of the locations of the bases were kept secret from us, undoubtedly with an interrogation like this in mind. I was surprised when he shook his head in a slow no.

'You will give me the information later. First you must be convinced of the seriousness of my aims. I intend to question you, then to enlist your services in our cause. Voluntarily. In order to convince you of this I must begin by saying you will not be killed. Strong men face death bravely. It is an easy escape from their problems. You have no such escape.'

I was becoming less and less intrigued all the time by what he had to say. I had expected a rough questioning session, but he had bigger things in mind. So I dropped the bantering tone and gave it to him straight.

'Forget it. Face the fact that I do not like you or your organization or what you stand for, and I do not intend to change my mind. Even if I promise to aid you you can never be sure that I meant it – so let us not get involved in this sort of farcical position to begin with.'

'Quite the contrary,' he said, and touched a button on his desk. The box above hummed and reeled in the thick wire pulling me upward until I had to stand on tiptoe in order to breathe, the collar biting into my neck. 'Before I am through with you you will be begging me for the opportunity to cooperate and will cry when I do not permit it, until you reach the happiest moment in your life when you are at last granted your single wish. Let me demonstrate one of our simpler but most convincing techniques.'

My feet vibrated with pain but I had to stay on my toes or I would have been strangled by the collar. Kraj rose and walked behind me where I could not see him – then seized both my wrists and pushed them down against the edge of the metal desk. The desk obliged him by snapping two cuffs about my wrists, clamping them there.

Not about my wrists, this isn't exactly true, but about my lower arm, leaving my wrists and hands free. Not that I could do anything more than drum my fingertips on the tabletop. Kraj reappeared and bent to take something from a drawer in the desk.

It was an ax. A long handled, steel edged ax of a primitive and efficient sort that could be used to chop

112

down trees. He took it in both hands and raised it high over his head.

'What are you doing? Stop!' I shouted in sudden fear, writhing in the metal embrace, unable to do anything except stare while he held the ax high for a moment. Then brought it down with a vicious, forceful chop.

I suppose I screamed when it hit, I must have, the pain was large and consuming.

As was the sight of my right hand severed from the wrist, lying unmoving on the desk top, the spout of blood from my wrist pumping out and drenching it. The ax went up again and this time I am sure I shouted aloud, screamed, all the time it went up and flashed down and my left hand was severed like the right and my life's blood spouted out all over the desk and ran down to the floor.

And through the pain and the terror that possessed me I was aware of Kraj's face. Smiling. Smiling for the first time.

Then I was unconscious. Blacking out, dying, I couldn't tell. The world rushed away from me down a dark tunnel and I was left with the sensation of pain alone and then even that was gone.

When I opened my eyes I was lying on the floor and a period of unmeasured time had gone by. My thoughts were thick with sleep or something else and I had to work to dredge up the memory of what had happened. Only when the startling vision of my severed hands came to me clearly did I open my eyes and sit up, rubbing one hand with the other. They felt perfectly normal. What had happened?

'Stand up,' Kraj's voice said, and I realized that I was sitting on the floor before his desk and that the collar was still in place about my neck with its wiring up to the device on the ceiling. I stood, slowly, and looked at his clean desk. There was no blood.

113

'I would have sworn . . . ' I said and my voice died away as I saw the two great grooves in the metal top of the desk as though it had been hit twice with some heavy blade. Then I lifted my hands before my face and looked at my wrists.

Each wrist was circled by a red weal of healing flesh with the sharp red points of removed stitches along the edges. Yet my hands felt as they always did. What had happened?

'Are you beginning to understand what I mean?' Kraj asked, once more seated behind the desk, his voice as gray as his clothing.

'What did you do? You couldn't have amputated my hands and sewed them back. I could tell, it would take time, you couldn't . . . ' I realized that I was starting to babble and I shut up.

'You don't believe it happened? Should I do it again?'

'No!' I said, almost shouting the word, drawing back from him. He nodded approvingly at this.

'So the training begins. You have lost a little bit of reality. You do not know what happened – but you do know that you do not wish it to happen again. This is the way it will go. Eventually you will lose all touch with the reality you have known all your life, and then will lose contact with the person you have been all your life. When you reach that state we will accept you as one of us. Then you will go into great detail about your Special Corps, not only racking your memory for crumbs of fact you may have missed, but in actively originating plans for their destruction.'

'It won't work,' I said with a great deal more sincerity than I really felt. 'I am not alone. The Corps is onto you now and actively working against you, so that it is now just a matter of time before they pull the plug and all your little invasion schemes go down the drain.'

'Quite the opposite,' Kraj said, clasping his hands together on the desk before him like a teacher about to lecture a class. 'We have been aware of their attention for a long time and have forestalled them at every turn. We have captured, tortured and killed a number of the Corps people to get information. We know that everything is geared to follow the lead of a field agent, such as yourself, and we have been waiting for one to come along. You have come, and we have you. It is that simple. You are the weapon with which we will destroy the Special Corps.'

He had me half believing him. The plan he proposed sounded like a reasonable one and I put that thought away as fast as it arrived. I was going to have to stop agreeing with him, attack rather than defend.

'That is very ambitious of you and I hope you don't bite off more than you can chew. Aren't you forgetting the hundreds of planets that support the league and what they can do to you when they find out the kind of trouble you are causing?'

'There are hundreds of planets only in theory, in reality they are just one after the other. We pluck them in that manner, they fall before us, we cannot be stopped, and the process is an accelerating one. As our empire expands we move faster and faster.'

'And there is a limit to that speed,' I broke in, trying to work a sneer into my words. 'I know how your invasion technique works. You don't invade a planet until they have already *lost*. Isn't that right?'

'Perfectly correct.' He nodded agreement and I rushed on.

'You find a planet that is ripe for the picking with some dissident element in the population; there are people who would complain about paradise so you have no problem in finding a group on any world. Here on Burada it was the

115

men, the Konsolosluk party. They were hot for male rule. You backed them with whatever they needed. Your underground operators supplied them with money, weapons, propaganda, all the essentials of a takeover – and it worked. And you asked nothing in return for all this aid, other than only a token resistance when the invasion began. Your agents saw to it that the armed forces surrendered after only the briefest show of force. This invasion was won before it began! No wonder your military people aren't used to taking losses.'

'Very observant of you. This is exactly what we do, your analysis is a masterly description of the way in which we operate.'

'Then I have you,' I said happily.

'On the contrary – we have you. You are the only one who knows about our techniques and you will never report them to your superiors.'

'Oh, I don't know,' I said with a bravado I did not feel.

'Perhaps you do not know, but we do. We have intercepted the report you made and it will never be sent. They will wait in vain for any work from you and time will pass and soon it will be too late for them to do anything because we will move into phase two of our operation. With the many allies we have gained by occupying planets with governments now friendly to us, we will have a considerable number of troops available to us. Mercenaries I believe they are called. They will be invasion troops and great numbers of them will be killed, but we will always win because our supply will be relatively inexhaustible. It presents an interesting picture, does it not?'

'It will never work,' I shouted, with the sinking feeling at the same time that it would. 'The Corps will stop you.' How, with their only agent run to earth and trapped? I was having a hard job convincing myself and getting nowhere at all in convincing him.

Kraj rose and started around the desk.

'Now it is time for your indoctrination to begin.'

I cannot express the fear that overwhelmed and possessed me when I heard those words.

CHAPTER FOURTEEN

I WAS TAKEN to a cell. A bare, windowless room whose only furnishing was an empty bucket. A ceiling hook had recently been installed here and my attendant gray man obligingly hooked me up to it.

'There is little chance of my starving to death,' I told him. 'Because I'll die of thirst first.'

He gave no spoken answer but he did return with a soft plastic water bottle and a standard Cliaand field ration. Not the world's most inspiring food, but it would keep me alive.

As I chewed and sipped I clamped hard on that last thought. Keep me alive. They would do anything except kill me. They wanted me, actually needed me. They knew that the Special Corps was breathing hot on their trail and they would have to exert an all-out effort to stop them. Kraj had talked big and half convinced me; I looked at my wrists and shuddered. He *had* convinced me. But why had he tried so hard?

Because I was obviously more than a pawn in this game. I was the factor that could swing the outcome either way. Right now Cliaand was doing well in the invasion business – but they could be stopped. With what I knew the Special Corps could start work as counter-insurgents and prevent expansion to other planets. Cliaand might even be stopped here. If I were to change sides my specialized knowledge might not defeat the Corps, but it could surely slow it down long enough for the second phase of the invasion operation to go into effect.

Which means the gray men had made a mistake. They

should have killed me as soon as they discovered who I was. If I could be tortured and convinced to change my mind I might be a weapon in their hands. Two maybes. That ignored the fact that as long as I was alive I was the most deadly and potent weapon against them.

They had made a mistake. I grabbed to that conclusion and worried it just as I worried the jaw-braking ration. I did not consider that I was their prisioner in every way. Every way? Ha! Physically, yes. Mentally – a resounding no. They had almost had me there for a while with the nerve torture and the positive assurance that I would fall into their hands. At the thought of amputation my stomach gave a heave and I suddenly lost my appetite. I had put the sight of my severed hands out of my mind. For good reasons.

Now I would have to remember and think about it. But not in the way they wanted. It was a trick, it *had* to be a trick, and that was the supposition I must hold on to. While I chewed and glugged down the rest of my unappetizing meal I gave myself the hard sell. Listen diGriz, you know enough about reality to be able to tell when it has been tampered with. You are always tampering with it yourself for your own benefit and others discommoding. So now someone has turned the same trick on you. *The severed wrists pumping blood*! Down, boy. Drain away some of the emotion. We'll get to the memories after a while. But let us look first at the realities.

Reality. Marvelous as medicine is it cannot repair amputation in a couple of hours or a couple of days.

Now where did that figure come from? At some unconscious level I felt that only a brief time had passed between the amputation and the recovery. We all have a clock ticking away down deep in the brain, it controls the circadian rhythms of sleeping and walking and it works all of the time. Right now it was trying to tell me

119

that only a brief time had passed since I had been brought here by the gray men. But did I have any real evidence to back it up? I felt my face and my hair. I needed a shave, but not badly, and my hair felt about the right length. But I could have had a haircut and a shave, no evidence there.

My fingernails? I kept them trimmed short, and one trimmed fingernail looks like any other one. Wait, think. Memory. Something. Small. Yes – during the landing, plenty of tension, plenty of distractions. I had broken the little fingernail on my left hand. No, don't look yet, sit on the thing and remember. Broken nail . . . distraction . . . bit it off. A rather unappetizing bit of self-consumption that most of us indulge in at one time or another. The offending particle of nail torn free, right down to the quick, a minor ouch and a tiny drop of blood. Completely forgotten in the rush of subsequent events.

With careful motions I released my left hand from its prisoning buttock and held it before me. Little finger, short nail – and a tiny clot of blood.

Got you, Kraj, you old faker!

From the look of the thing I had been a prisoner for a day or two at the most, surely no longer than that. The red marks on my wrists were just that – red marks on my wrists. There were a hundred different ways this could have been done. And the amputation? Kraj had tampered with my reality, hypnosis perhaps, it didn't really matter.

Kraj and his crew were not as bright as they looked. They had undoubtedly used this mind-cracking torture many times before and had really impressed themselves with the success of the technique. Perhaps this was the way they converted recruits to their nasty ends on the planets they were to invade. Very possible. But Kraj's cutthroats were used to working on solid citizens, one dimensional peasants who mistook the painted flats and props of their existence as the only reality. Their world was the only real world, their town the really best town. Pull them out of the familiar environment and put pressure on their minds and their brains ran out of their ears like jelly. Jelly men, prey for the gray men.

Not noble, upright, flexible, dishonest, chameleon-like Slippery Jim diGriz. Man of a thousand faces, familiar of a hundred cultures, linguistically competent in scores of tongues. And they wanted to louse up *my* reality? It made me laugh. I laughed.

I not only laughed but I scampered and danced. I ran in circles shouting Yippee! and Victory! and other cries of happiness. Because of my collar and cable I was forced to run in circles but I found that I could vary this by swinging in circles. The cable was too thin to climb, deliberately designed so I am sure, but I could coil a loop of it and hang from this. I made the loop as high above my head as I could reach, grabbed it, kicked off and swung freely. At the bottom of the swing I kicked hard and went higher. Great fun. Until my hand slipped and the loop unlooped.

Everything almost ended at that moment as all of my weight came on the metal collar about my neck. That's the the way they kill people, you know, by hanging. Not by suffocating them. By giving that sudden jerk to the noose that breaks the spinal cord.

This thought was uppermost in my mind as I clutched and scrabbled at the cable and managed to grip it before the snap came. And it came on the front of my neck, not the side, or I might very well have heard that sharp *crack* that signals the end. It hurt and everything went around in circles for a minute and when I said *Wow*! it was in a whispered voice because I had not done my vocal cords any good either.

Eventually I sat up and drank some water and felt a

little better – and wondered why no one had come to investigate all the recent nonsense. I was sure they had the room bugged to watch me, but perhaps they were not impressed by my acrobatics. Or maybe they were so busy with the invasion that they did not have time to keep that careful an eye on me. If this latter supposition were correct, then perhaps I might be able to capitalize on it.

The food wrappings and the water bottle wadded together to make excellent padding for my hands. Around this I wrapped a double loop of the cable, close against my neck. Then, clutching the cable tightly, I jumped as high as I could and let my weight crash down on the cable.

And on my arms. By the tenth time I had done this I was beginning to feel as though my arms would be torn off at the sockets before any vital part of my emprisoning mechanism gave way. The theory was certainly sound enough. A metal box, a cable, a handle, a hook, a number of components the failure of any one of which might grant freedom. Though my components were failing much faster. I panted a bit, wiped my forehead with my forearm, and jumped up for try number thirteen.

Lucky thirteen! Something snapped with a sharp metallic crack and the box came down and bounced off my head.

I was out, how long I don't know, probably only a few moments, and came to shaking my head and trying to stand. *Move* was the pressing thought, get out of here before they came for me. But first I had to deactivate the torture box since it could be worked by remote radio control. I turned it over and saw that the metal loop by which it was suspended had fractured. There was a control section here with about 50 small red buttons arranged in a grid. I shivered at the thought of pressing any of them. Above the grid were two large buttons, one red, one black. The red was depressed. This seemed obvious enough. Logically I should push the black one and turn the box off, but memories of the pain kept intruding. Finally I stabbed down on the black button.

Nothing happened. That I could feel. With this security I lightly touched one of the small red buttons, then another and another. Nothing. The box was now so much dead metal. I hoped. I coiled up the extra cable until the box dangled handily. Then tried the door. Which proved to be unlocked. Inefficient warders or great faith in their torture machines. Putting my eyes close to the edge of the door I opened it a crack.

And closed it even more swiftly. Coming down the corridor towards me were two of the gray men carrying a sinister looking object between them. I had not seen enough of it to capture any details, though what I had seen had given me a definitely crawling sensation. The next step in the diGriz pacification program? This seemed highly probable when the door handle started to turn.

There was a surprise in store for this pair and I wanted to keep it from them as long as I could. As the door opened I stepped behind it and waited while they struggled with the bulky torture machine. Only when I heard one of them gasp in alarm did I put my shoulder to the door and ram it into them with all my weight and strength. As soon as they crunched and howled I jumped around the door, the metal control box swinging at the end of its cable.

One of them was bent over, more interested in the weight of the machine on his foot than in anything else and I let my weapon bounce off the top of his skull. While it rebounded the second man tried for his gun and actually had it halfway out of its holster before my knee caught him low in the stomach and he folded on top of his associate. I plucked the gun from his limp fingers as he went down and now I was armed.

During most of my stay in the building I had been conscious and I thought I knew my way out. Back through the main entrance which was sure to be guarded. It was one flight down and in the opposite direction from Kraj's chambers. The gausspistol had a full charge of power and a filled magazine as well. There was no time to check what kind of ammunition it was loaded with, but it was surely something lethal which was fine by me. I was in a lethal mood. I wrapped the cable up close to the box so it wouldn't swing and get in my way, took a deep breath – and dived out of the door.

The hallway was empty, a good beginning. I trotted to the stairs without seeing anyone, then went down them two at a time. The next floor would be the ground floor since they had only taken me up one storey. This memory was opposed by the reality that there was a rather large stairwell beside me that did not end at the next floor. When this fact finally registered on my tardy synapses I skidded to a stop and looked carefully over the edge of the railing.

There were at least eight more stories below this one.

They had been running through my cerebral cortex with their little leaden boots. This certainly proved my theoretical stance that a good deal of what had happened to me was illusion or false memory. What had been real? Was this 'escape' real at the present moment? This was a chilling thought; everything that was happening could be a generated series of unreal events to prove to me that I could not escape. I could keep going down these stairs forever or wake up at any moment back in my room still attached to my pendant box. Well, if this were true, there was absolutely nothing I could do about it. I had to treat this illusion like reality until it proved otherwise. Unless this was an endless dream building these stairs had to end somewhere, and I was going to find out.

Four floors down, just when I was beginning to get dizzy from the constant circling, I met another man coming up. A gray man with a rifle and a very surprised look. Since I had been expecting this encounter and he hadn't I got in the first shot.

Quite a shot. The gausspistol was loaded with explosive slugs. They blasted a gaping hole in the staircase and hurled the gray man against the wall where he slumped, crumpled and unconscious. The echoes were still booming and the dust unsettled when I leaped the gaping hole and hurled myself down the stairs at a suicidal pace. It would be more certain suicide to wait around.

The stairs ended, I was at the bottom, and I slammed into the wall I was going so fast. There was much shouting from above me and the hammer of running feet. My gun at the ready I pushed open the door and walked into blackness.

It was a bit of a shock and I almost fired off a couple of rounds on general principle but, as my eyes adjusted, I saw a dim light in the distance. There were rough walls and dust and other indications that I had bypassed the ground floor and ended up in a cellar. Which was all right too since there was undoubtedly a warm reception waiting for me a flight above. If I could get out of the basement I was still one jump ahead of the competition. Gun ready, metal box swinging, shins bruised by unseen obstacles, I stumbled towards the far off light. I was not enthused when I reached towards the far off light. I was not enthused when I reached it after running the invisible obstacle course. It was a window.

But a small window, high on the wall, coated with insect corpses and dirt. And heavily barred.

Behind me in the darkness there were shouts, running

feet, crashing noises and healthy curses. What to do?

Obvious. Get out. I stepped back, raised the gun, shielded my face, and blew the window out. And part of the wall around it and some of the street outside until my gun clicked empty. I dropped it, slung my box over my shoulder and used my free hand to help me scrabble up the slope of rubble and out into the street.

To start running again. Someone saw me and shouted but I did not shout back. I ran harder even though I was getting winded and more than a little fatigued by the effort. It is one thing to escape, it is another thing altogether to stay free once out. Barefooted, dressed in totally transparent clothes with a collar and some meters of wire about my neck, not to mention the control box, I must have presented a rather unusual and unmistakable sight. I needed to hide, hole up, change, get rid of the collar, a lot of things. And I was getting very tired.

I went around a corner as fast as I could and slammed into someone coming in the opposite direction. We both went down and I rolled on my back like a bug, near exhaustion, gasping for air. Then I saw the face of the man I had run into and had a last little burst of hope.

'Ostrov,' I gasped. 'Old friend, old roommate, old co-pilot. I am in trouble and need your help. The locals, you see . . . '

I saw Ostrov, a mild man at the worst of times, turn into a very angry animal. Twisted face, bulging eyes, the works. He dived on me and pinned me to the cold ground.

'Locals nothing,' he shouted. 'Kraj has been asking after you. Kraj wants you. What have you done?'

CHAPTER FIFTEEN

I STRUGGLED A BIT, but it did me no good. My heart wasn't in it and I was close to exhaustion. Though I did manage to catch my ex-friend Ostrov a good one on the side of the head with my torture box. His eyes crossed but he didn't let go and by that time a small squad of gray men were upon us, peeling him off and prodding me to my feet with their rifle barrels. I prodded slowly. Sunk in dark despair and limp with fatigue I was certainly in no hurry.

There were six of them and Ostrov, who had a look on his face of wishing to be elsewhere.

'Kraj talked to me, you see. About Vaska here, said he wanted him . . . ' His voice ran down and expired when the stoney faced men completely ignored him. I didn't.

'What did you expect – gratitude? You rat. Starting your own bowb-your-buddy week, aren't you?' I tried to sneer but it turned to a gurgle when one of my captors jerked on my cable. One of my five captors. I blinked and looked again because I could swear there had been six there a moment ago.

While I was still counting a pair of hands reached up and closed around the neck of number five. His eyeballs bulged and his mouth gaped and I worked to keep my expression calm and not to bulge my own eyes in the same manner. The hands scrunched, the eyes closed, and number five vanished from sight. I struggled a bit so the survivors would keep their attention on me, even lashing out a foot and getting Ostrov in the ankle to keep him occupied as well.

'You didn't have to do that,' he complained. I smiled as number four went the way of the others.

There was something to be admired in the efficient and quiet disposal of the enemy. It reminded me of a hunter I once worked with on a planet whose name I forget. He was a professional and very good at his job. He would go out at dawn when a flock of birds was going over and shoot the last bird in the flight. Then the next one and the next one. He could get four or five sometimes without the other birds even knowing what was happening. The same principle was being applied here in an equally professional way.

The system broke down with number four who thrashed a bit and drew the attention of one of the others, human beings being slightly smarter than birds after all. I waited until they had turned towards the disturbance then let the nearest gray man have it in the side of the neck with the edge of my hand. Fatigue weakened the blow so that he didn't drop at once and I had to let him have a few more to quiet him. And while I worked I was aware of thuds and cut-off screams from the others.

When I straightened up I saw that Ostrov and all but one of the gray men were dozing happily in a heap, while my rescuers put down the final one. He was a big bruiser and fought well, but he was outclassed and soon unconscious. Which was interesting because both of his attackers were women – dressed in skimpy and colorful Burada shifts and high-heeled local shoes. The nearest one turned and I recognized Sergeant Taze and some of the pieces began to fall into place.

The other woman was smaller and quite neatly formed, with a figure I remembered and a face I could not forget. My wife.

'There, there,' Angelina said, patting me on one cheek and giving me a quick kiss on the other. 'I hope you can run a bit darling, because more of these thugs are on the way.' A projectile of some kind whined by to punctuate the statement.

'Run . . .' I said hoarsely and staggered off, still not quite sure what had happened but at least still bright enough to not ask any questions. Taze put her arm around me, getting me going in the right direction and pulling me along, while my Angelina relieved me of the weight of box and cable. We rushed away like that and I'm sure we made a charming sight, me in my transparent coveralls and the girls in their neat little frocks, except no one was on the street to appreciate the scene.

'Keep going!' Taze shouted as she dragged me around a corner. There were explosions close behind us. I ignored everything except putting one foot in front of the other as fast as I could and wondered just how long I would last.

Taze seemed to know what she was doing. Before we had gone very far in this new direction she turned, half carried me up a few steps and into a building. She threw the bolts on the heavy door and we staggered on, a little slower now, through deserted offices of some kind, to the rear where the windows faced on a courtyard. There was a good sized drop here and Taze went first, lithe as a big cat, then helped me down with Angelina lowering from above. I was as putty in their hands, and a very nice sensation it was too. Taze ran ahead to open a large door. Inside was a Cliaand command car with a general's flag still flying from the antenna.

'That's more like it,' I said, walking over on rubbery legs.

'In the back you two,' Taze ordered, pulling on a military jacket and pushing her hair up under a Cliaand helmet. I did not ask what had happened to the original owner. Angelina was right behind me when I crawled into the back and collapsed on the floor, snuggling her warm round curves up against me. I felt very comfortable as the car bounced forward. I enjoyed a good hug and a kiss before I could get in any questions.

'Your figure has improved,' I managed to gasp when I came up for air.

'You'll be so happy to know that you are now the proud father of twins. Both boys. With big mouths and hearty appetites like their father. I've named them James and Bolivar after you.'

'Anything you say, my sweet. I suppose you would not mind telling me how you came to be here at this most opportune moment?'

'I came to take care of you, and as you can see I was right.'

'Yes, of course,' I said, and nodded dimly at this fine bit of female logic. 'Mechanically, I mean. The last I saw you were headed for the hospital with a bulge in your midriff and the light of motherhood in your eyes.'

'Well that all worked out fine as I've told you, weren't you listening? Then I heard that these filthy Cliaand people were off to invade another planet and that you were probably taking part in the invasion.'

'Inskipp told you all this?'

'Of course not!' She sniffed delicately at the thought. 'I broke into his files and found the records. He was very angry but did not try to stop me when I came here with the follow-up team. I imagine he knew better than to interfere. In fact he promised to keep an eye on the nurse and the children for me. We went into orbit, received the message and I came down, that's about all there is to it. Let me try this lockpick on that horrid collar thing you're

130

wearing. I don't know why you ever let them treat you like this.'

'There are one or two gaps in your story,' I insisted. 'Like what message?'

'My message,' Taze said, who had been shamelessly eavesdropping while she drove. 'You forget that I am a sergeant in the Guard and I had seen the message you prepared, the one they took away. So of course I had memorized it as well as the radio frequencies. Those swine took me to a prison camp for *civilians* so I left it that same night.' Taze was quite sure of herself and, looking back at the record, I realized she had cause to be.

'I came down in a scout ship as soon as the call was heard.' Angelina diddled with the lockpick while she talked. 'I had to shoot my way in which certainly was not hard to do. For galaxy conquerors these people are very indifferent pilots. Then I met Taze.' Angelina touched her lips to my ear and hissed coldly. 'How well do you know this girl?' She twisted the collar at the same time.

'Just met her that once,' I gasped, and the pressure let off. 'Not my type at all.'

'You like them buxom like that, don't lie to me Jim diGriz.'

I blinked rapidly and tried to restore the conversation to its original direction.

'But then, how did you find me? What did you do?'

'Simple enough.' There was a click and the collar snapped open. I rubbed my sore neck with relief. 'There is only one building where these men in gray uniforms operate. We watched it, trying to find a way in. Our only trouble was the soldiers, trying to pick us up all the time. But we extracted information from them. And this car.'

I had a vision of these two murderous cuties slowly decimating the Cliaanlian invasion with their own secret weapons, and knew enough not to ask about the fate of the driver and his friends.

'Now tell us what happened to you,' Angelina said, and snuggled down to hear a good story. 'I'm dying to find out what this thing is they had on your neck and why in heaven you are wearing that awful transparent suit.'

I told them all right, and was rewarded with a number of girlish gasps, and at least one screech when I got to the wrist part. Taze even stopped the car so she could look at the scars too. After that they listened in cold-eyed stillness and I almost felt sorry for any of the gray men they might meet in the future. By the time I had finished my fascinating and slightly repulsive story we had arrived at wherever we were going. A wide door opened at our approach and closed behind us. Other girls were there, well armed and attractive for the most part, and I wondered how the Konsolosluk party had ever managed to muster up a resistance to a government like this. Thank the Cliaandians for that. When it comes to governments and armies I'm pretty much of an anarchist and think least is best in both departments. But if you have to have them it sure helps if they are pretty. I shook my head, and let myself be led to a room where there was a very enticing army cot. I dropped onto it.

'Clothes,' I said, 'and drink, and not necessarily in that order.' I tucked a corner of the blanket coyly over me. not out of shame, rather that these alert amazons should not be subject to temptation. And besides, my wife was there. She knew very well what I meant by drink and pushed aside the glass of water one of the ladies was trying to force on me and passed over a small flask of potent brew. It burned sweetly down my throat and sent tendrils of fire into my brain.

'I'm afraid my thoughts . . . my sense of reality is still a little confused,' I admitted, and from the look on

Angelina's face I knew that she was already aware of it. 'They did something to me, don't know what, but it'll wear off soon I'm sure.'

'I'll kill them, every one, terribly,' Angelina said through tight-clenched teeth and there was a murmur of agreement from all the listeners. I closed my eyes for a moment to rest them and when I opened them again the room was empty except for Angelina; a light had been lit and the window was dark. It was like a spliced break in a film with a chunk left out. I respected Kraj's mental diddling techniques and roundly loathed him for it.

'Hungry,' I told Angelina and she came over and sat by me and held my hand.

'You've been asleep – and talking. Some awfully strange things.'

'I feel better for it. When we get back to base I'll have the medics vacuum out all the dark corners. But there are more important things for the present. We have to organize the resistance here before the Cliaand get a tight grip on everything. And ...'

'No.'

'What do you mean *no*?'

I had the feeling that I had missed some important part of the conversation. Was this more results of the brain diddling – or just female conversation?

'I mean no, we won't do that. While you were sleeping I sent a long report to Inskipp, everything you told me about the Cliaand plans and how they work their invasions and how they are out to get the Corps, everything.'

'Did you at least sign my name?' I asked, petulantly.

She patted my hand. 'Of course, darling. It was *your* work and I wouldn't *think* of trying to get credit for it.'

I was filled with instant regret for speaking like that, and apologized, then she apologized because my ill temper probably had to do with the brain business, and we had a

133

drink and that was settled and I tried to get back to the business at hand.

'So you sent the report. And then—?'

'Then it went to a relay ship on the other side of this sun and was sent out as a psigram to Inskipp. His answer came in and he said "message received, congratulations, return at once". So you see you will have to go back.'

I snorted through my nose, then sipped my drink.

'Do you think I'll go back?'

'You're not well, you need medical attention, you've done what you came to do—'

'That's not what I asked. Do *you* think I'll go back now?'

Angelina tried to look fierce, which she cannot do unless she really means it – then shrugged her shoulders in a very resigned way.

'Of course not. If you did you would not be the man I married. So now we wipe out these fiends and save Burada and stop these invasions.'

'Not quite all at once, but that is sort of what I had in mind. A resistance movement will have to be organized, with our advice and material help Taze should be able to handle that, but there is one thing that takes priority over even that. We must capture Kraj or one of his gray men.'

'What a wonderful idea! If they think they know about torture they will soon learn a thing or two. I remember . . .'

'Angelina! That is not what I had in mind. For a moment there a lot of the old reconstructed you was shining through.'

'Nonsense. I admit I could use one or two techniques I learned in those days, but my motives are the purest. Lioness defending her mate and that sort of thing. Perfectly justified.'

'Yes, that might be so, but it is not quite what I was talking about. I want one of those gray men in a laboratory and I want exhaustive tests run on him. When you were beating up on that bunch earlier today did you notice anything strange about them?'

'Nothing particular. I was otherwise occupied, you might say. Just the fact that they weren't wearing enough clothing, because their skins felt so chill.'

'Exactly so. And they never laugh or show emotion, they don't gossip or talk unless there is something important to say, and have a number of other little traits that draw the attention.'

'Just what are you trying to say, darling, that they are zombies or robots or something? I thought that sort of thing appeared only on space operas for the kiddies.'

'Laugh now, while there is still time. Not robots or such, these types are alive enough. I just don't think that they are human, that's all. There are aliens among us.'

'Perhaps you better have some more sleep. I'll turn down the light.'

'Don't humor me, damn it! I have been thinking about this ever since I first met Kraj, so it is no figment of a recently tortured mind. There is all sort of evidence. The Cliaand soldiers are deathly afraid of Kraj and his thugs and won't even talk about them. The gray men are cut off from normal Cliaandian life and different in every way from them. Almost as though they were not the same people. I can visualize these gray men doing a survey of the human planets and finding Cliaand just ripe for their picking. A stratified, militarized way of life with everyone in uniform. All they had to do was take over at the top and they would be in control. And this they seem to have done. They appear in none of the tables or charts so dear to the military mind – yet they seem to be running things most of the time.'

'Well . . .'

'There. You're not convinced but you are beginning to doubt. Then you'll help me get a specimen gray man?'

'Help?' She clapped her hands with sheer girlish enthusiasm. 'I am simply looking forward to it. Of course he might get a little damaged while I'm bringing him in, but as long as he still works that is really all that matters, isn't it?'

Before I could answer Taze ran in and threw an armload of clothing onto the bed.

'Get dressed, quickly,' she ordered. 'The boots are the biggest we could find and I hope they fit.'

'Is there any reason for all this rush?' I asked.

'There certainly is. There are troops and heavy weapons on all sides. This building is completely surrounded by the enemy.'

CHAPTER SIXTEEN

THE BOOT WAS TIGHT and delicately pointed, but I squeezed my foot in as far as I could. 'Were we followed here?' I asked Taze.

'No – of course not. I am no beginner at this business. Nor is the stolen car here any longer.'

I cudgeled my sluggish brain into thought while I struggled with the second boot. The telephone rang and I froze – as did the two women – staring at it like a poison snake. It rang just once more, then the tiny inset screen lit up and Kraj stared out of it, as emotionless as ever.

'You know that you are surrounded,' he said. 'Resistance is useless, diGriz. Surrender quietly and none of your friends will be hurt . . .'

My boot hit the screen and Kraj's image flared and died; I ripped the entire instrument out by the roots and hurled it against the wall. A fine cold sweat dotted my skin. I knew that most phones can be turned on from central with the right equipment, but this was a bad time to see the theory proven.

'Don't panic!' I shouted, mostly to myself I imagine, because Angelina and Taze were perfectly calm. I hopped about the room getting on the other boot and tried to jar some clear thought into my tangled brain. The last hop ended me up sitting on the cot, panting, counting off on my fingers.

'Let us forget that call for a moment and figure out what is happening. One, we were not followed when we came here. Two, our transportation is gone so that we could not be traced. Three, Kraj knew that I was here, which means they may have planted a directional radio transmitter in me. In which case the services of a surgeon and a good x-ray machine will be needed as soon as we get out of here.'

'You are forgetting a simpler explanation,' Angelina said.

'Don't keep it a secret. If you can think better than I can – which is no compliment right now – let's have it.'

'The torture box. You said it was radio controlled.'

'Of course. A directional apparatus is probably an integral part of the mechanism. Is the thing still here, Taze?'

'Yes, below. We thought there might be a use for it.'

'There is now. When we leave the box stays here. Maybe this will keep their attention on the building – and once away they won't find me this easily again. Now brief me, Taze, what kind of a building is this – and how do we get out of it?'

'It is a factory owned by one of our members. And there is no possible way out, we are doomed to fight and die, but when we do we will sell our lives well and take many of those swine-pig-dogs with us . . .'

'That's fine, yes indeed. But we'll sell our lives dearly only if we have to. DiGriz can find escape routes where others only despair. Is your factory owner here? Good, send her up as quickly as possible.'

Taze left on a run and I turned to my wife.

'I assume you brought the usual equipment with you? The sort of thing we had on our honeymoon.'

'Bombs, grenades, explosives, gas charges, of course.'

'Good girl. With you for a wife I have a growing sense of security.'

Taze ran back in followed by another uniformed amazon. A little older perhaps, with a very attractive touch of gray to her hair, yet full-bosomed and round-limbed in a maturely fascinating way . . . I caught the cold look frosting in Angelina's eyes and quickly put my thoughts on more pressing matters.

'I am James diGriz, interstellar spy and agent.'

'Fayda Firtina of the Guard,' she barked and snapped a salute.

'Yes, very good, Fayda, glad to meet you. At ease. I understand that you own this building.'

'That is correct. Firtina Amalgamated (construction) Robutlers, Limited. The finest product on the market.'

'What is?'

'Robutlers.'

'You wouldn't think me dense if I asked what a Robutler is?'

'A luxury product that is a necessity for the proper home. A robot that is programmed, trained, articulated and specially designed for but a single function. A butler, a servant, a willing aid around the house that makes the house a home, relieving the lady of the establishment of the chores and cares and stresses of modern living . . .'

There was more like this, obviously quotes from a sales brochure, but I did not hear it. A plan was forming in my mind, taking shape – until the sound of firing broke through my train of thought.

'They have made a probing attack,' Taze said, a com-radio to her ear. 'But were repulsed with losses.'

'Keep holding them. They shouldn't try the heavy stuff for a while since they hope to get me alive.' I waved over the factory owner who seemed ready to go on with her sales talk. 'Fayda, will you give me a quick sketch of the ground plan of the building and the immediate area around it.'

She drew quickly and accurately, military training no doubt, indicating doors and windows and the surrounding streets.

'What do your robutlers look like?' I asked.

'Roughly humanoid in form and size, the optimum shape for a home environment. In addition—'

'That's fine. How many do you have ready to go, field tested or whatever you call it, with their little power packs charged?'

She frowned in thought. 'I'll have to check with shipping, but at a rough guess I would say between 150 and 200.'

'That will be just perfect for our needs. Would you be terribly put out – your insurance might cover it – if they were destroyed in the cause of Burada freedom?'

'Every Firtina robutler would willingly die, happily, if it had any emotions, for the cause. Though of course they are incapable of bearing arms or of violent acts of any kind.'

'They don't have to. We can take care of that. Our robutler brigade will be the diversion that gets us out of here. Now come close, girls, and I'll tell you the plan.'

The old diGriz brain was really turning over at last. The firing in the background only stimulated me to grander efforts, while I was buoyed up on a wave of cheerful enthusiasm. Within minutes the preparations were being made, and within a half an hour the robots were ready to attack.

'You know your orders?' I asked the dimly lit shipping bay full of robots.

'That we do sir, yes sir, thank you sir,' they all answered in the best of cultured accents.

'Then prepare to depart. What you do now is a far far better thing than you would have ever done in an electronic lifetime of domestic service. When I say leave you will leave, each to its appointed task.'

'Very kind sir, thank you sir.'

There were over a hundred here in the shipping bay of the factory, our main diversionary attack. They stood in neat rows, humming and eager to go. The front ranks were dressed in the excess garments we had been able to assemble; some with uniform hats, others with jackets, still fewer wearing slacks. Most of the clothing had been donated piecemeal by the female shocktroops, which fact was not doing me much good in my new marital status. There was entirely too much tanned flesh around for a man to completely ignore. It was almost a pleasure to be with the robots for a change. Their forms were sleek but hard, their dress inconsistent and revealing nothing of interest. And each of them clutched a length of pipe or plastic or some other object resembling a weapon. In the confusion that was soon to come my hope was that they would be mistaken for human attackers. I looked at my watch and raised the comradio to my mouth.

'Stand by, all units. Fifteen seconds to zero. Bombers stand ready. Keep away from the windows until the last second. Ready, keep low . . . trigger your bombs . . . *THROW*.'

There was a series of dull explosions from the street outside, that would be echoed on all sides of the building, as the girls heaved the bombs from the upper stories. Smoke bombs for the most part, though there were some irritants and sleep gas mixed in with them. I gave the bombs five seconds to maximum density, then hit the garage door switches. The doors rumbled up to reveal little other than twisting coils of smoke that instantly began to pour into the garage.

'Go, my loyal troops, go!' I ordered and every left foot shot forward as one, and the ranks of my robot brigade surged forward.

'Thanking *you*, sir!' mellifluously sounded in perfect tones from those metallic throats, and I retreated as they ran by.

There was firing now, from the windows above, echoed instantly by the troops outside. According to plan. I looked at my watch as I ran. Fifteen seconds from zero, time for the second wave.

'All other robutler units – *now*' I ordered into the comradio.

At that moment, from the other doors and exits of the factory, into the shroud of smoke and gas, the remaining robots should be going into action. I had not taken the time to try and rig an eavesdropping circuit on the enemy's command net, but I could just imagine what was happening now. What I hoped was happening now.

The building was surrounded, all their troops alert, our stronghold visible in all details in the warm afternoon sunlight. Then the sudden change, smoke, chemical irritants, shrouding the building on all sides. A breakout obviously – and there it was! Dim figures in the smoke, firing, get them, shoot to kill. Zoing, zoing! Take that, you rotten Burada guerrilla fink! What fighters these Burada are – men of steel! – shoot them and they don't fall. Panic in the smoke. The word that there are other breakouts. Which was the real one, which a cover? How to mass the troops? Where should the reserves be sent?

I figured that it would take about one minute for the first confusion to have reached its peak. After this the smoke would begin to thin and the dead bodies would be discovered to be robots and the word would get out. We wanted to get out before this word did. Once the bombs had been thrown Taze and her troops would be hurrying to get into position – and one minute was not very much time to reach the back of the factory from the upper floors. Yet most of them were there before me with Taze checking them off as they ran past.

'That's the lot,' she said, making a final tick on her list. '*Now*! Angelina, stand ready with the grenades.'

The small exit was unlocked and dragged open and Angelina hurled her smoke grenades out to intensify the gloom before us. There was no more talking, and in the sudden silence the shooting and shouting could clearly be heard. I was sure that I could detect an occasional *Thank you sir* among the voices. Fayda led the way and we followed in line, hands on the shoulders of the preceding marchers. I was in the middle of the line and Angelina just before me, so I held on to her. The placement was accidental, I am sure, since she wouldn't have cared if I clutched one of the half-naked Burada cuties.

It was a little disconcerting moving helplessly like this through the darkness, particularly when the occasional missile whined past. By accident, I hoped. This street was narrow and blocked at both ends by Cliaand troops. If they knew what was happening they could sweep the street with a deadly crossfire. But hopefully they were involved with the robutlers for the moment. All we had to do was quietly cross the 20 meters or so of open road, to the apartment dwelling on the other side. If we reached this unnoticed we had a good chance of going through it to the mixed business and residential plaza on the other side. From here we would break up and scatter through the warren of streets and walkways and tunnels, hopefully merging into the civilian population and disappearing before our absence was noticed. Hopefully.

I was counting my steps so knew I had almost reached the building – which meant that half of our number were safe – when the voice called out nearby.

'Is that you, Zobno? What did the sergeant say about robots? It sounded like robots?'

The line stopped, instantly, in breath-holding silence. We were so close. The voice was male and it spoke Cliaandian.

'Robots? What robots?' I asked as I pulled the hand from my shoulder and placed it on Angelina's shoulder before me. '*Move*,' I whispered in her ear. Then left the line and stamped heavily towards him in my new boots.

'I'm sure he said robots,' the voice complained. Behind me I was aware of the faint stir as the line started forward again. I stamped and coughed and moved closer to the unseen speaker. My hands before me ready for a quick clench and crush as soon as he spoke again.

All of which would have worked fine, and have given me a little sadistic pleasure, if the evening breeze had not sent eddies around the corners of the building. The wind moved coolly on my face and a rift opened in the smoke. I was looking at a Cliaand trooper, helmed and armed with his gaussrifle at the ready, a shocked expression stamped on his face. With good reason. Instead of gazing upon a fellow trooper he saw an unknown individual with snapping fingers, red eyes and unshaven jaw, dressed in totally transparent dungarees and ladies' boots, with bundles and packs slung on his shoulders. Gape was about all he could do.

This paralysis lasted just long enough for me to reach him. I grabbed him by the throat so he couldn't shout a warning, and by the gun so he couldn't shoot me. We danced around like this for a bit and the smoke closed over us again. My opponent wasn't shouting or shooting – but neither was he submitting. He was burly and well muscled and holding his own. Luckily he wasn't too bright and kept both his hands on the gun and tried to get it away from me. Just about the time he realized he could hold it with one hand and slug me with the other I got a foot behind his heel and went down on top of him. Before he hit the ground he managed to get two quick punches into my midriff which did me no good. Then we landed and I knocked all the air out of him. This freed my throat hand and, before he could suck in enough breath to shout with, I rendered him unconscious.

I sat on him, waiting for my head to stop spinning and

for the knot of pain in my gut to ease, when another voice sounded.close by.

'What's that noise? Who is it?'

I breathed in a deep shuddering breath, let a bit of it out and worked for control of my voice.

'It's me.' Always a good answer. 'I tripped and fell down. I hurt a finger . . .'

'Then you'll get a medal for it. Now shut up.'

I shut up, took the gaussrifle from my limp companion and stood up – and realized that I was completely lost in the smoky darkness.

Not a pleasant sensation at all. The smoke was thinning and I was alone with no sense of direction. If I walked in the wrong direction it would be suicide.

Panic! Or rather a moment of panic. I always allow myself at least a brief panic in any tight situation. This flushes out the bloodstream, starts the heart pumping faster, releases a jolt of adrenalin and provides other nice things for an emergency. But only a little panic, time was pressing. And after the basic bestial emotion drained away, lips dropped back over fangs and hair on neck down again and all that, I put the old logic center to work.

ITEM: I was not alone. The silent line of escapees may have marched into the building and safety, but my Angelina would not desert me. I knew, as clearly as if I could see her, that she was outside that door to survival and waiting for me.

ITEM: She had her sense of direction, I didn't. Therefore she would have to come to me.

'This finger is killing me, Sarge,' I whined, then whistled in supposed agony. One short whistle and one long one. The letter a for Angelina in the code that I knew she knew well. That I needed help I knew she would figure out for herself.

'Stop that whistling and noise,' the other voice growled back, ending in a note of suspicion. 'Say, who are you?'

I groped through my memory for the name I had heard a few moments earlier.

'It's me, Sarge. Zobno. This finger . . .'

'That's not Zobno!' a second voice called out. 'I'm Zobno . . .'

'No, *I* am,' I shouted. 'Who's that said that?'

'Both of you come here – *now!*' the sergeant ordered. 'I'm going to start shooting in five seconds.'

The real Zobno stumbled through the smoke and I didn't dare say a thing or move. And I could already feel the slugs tearing through me – when something plucked at my sleeve and I jumped.

'Angelina?' I whispered, and received a silent answer when she threw her arms about me. I reached for her but she wasn't waiting; taking my hand she pulled me after her. There were voices behind us in the smoke, then the sudden whine of a gaussrifle and shouts of command.

I stumbled over an invisible step and waiting hands pulled me through the doorway.

CHAPTER SEVENTEEN

'SEARCH PARTY . . . search party . . .'

The words came dimly through the throaty growls of the attacking teddy bears. I could have fought them off, even though the candy canes I was using for swords kept breaking on me. But even without a candy cane give a teddy a quick kick in the gut and over he goes, no staying power. The teddies I could have handled alone if they hadn't got those damn wooden soldiers on their side. They would make a good bonfire and that is just what I had in mind, fumbling for matches, when one of them got me in the arm with the bayonet on his toy rifle. It stung and I blinked and opened my eyes to look up at the whiskery face of Doctor Mutfak who was staring back at me.

'An alarm, that was, very badly timed indeed I must say. I have given you an injection to cancel the hypnotic drug.' He held up the hypodermic and I rubbed my arm where it had stung me. 'Very badly timed.'

'I didn't arrange it that way,' I mumbled, still only half awake and wishing I could have finished off the teddy bears.

'The treatment is going well and it will be time consuming to start over again. I have regressed you to your childhood and – my! – you have had an interesting, not to say repellent childhood! You must give me permission to write up this case. The symbol of the teddy bear, normally one of warmth and comfort, has been transmogrified by your obnoxious subconscious into . . .'

'Later, doctor, if you please,' Angelina said, coming to

my rescue. A picture of golden charm, she had been sunning herself on the balcony and the wisps of fabric she wore for this operation had about the same surface area as a butterfly's wing.

I sat up and shook my head, still foggy with the traces of the drug. The room was colorful and luxurious, with one entire wall opening onto the balcony, with the blue sky and bluer ocean beyond, perched high on top of the Ringa Baligi Hotel. This hotel, supposed to be the best one on Burada and I could well believe it, was in the center of a lagoon and approachable only by water or air. This gave us advance warning of any unwanted visitors – and the warning had just been given. The drill was carefully worked out. I had worn swim trunks during the brain-bending session, just in case of an emergency like this one, so I took Angelina's hand and we trotted to the private elevator. As we got into it the sound of engines on the landing platform above was loud and clear. We held the grips as the high-speed elevator dropped out from under us.

'Do you feel up to this?' Angelina asked.

'Just a bit foggy, but that will go away. Do you think this brain-drainer is any good?'

'He's supposed to be the best on the planet. He'll straighten out the kinks Kraj put in if anyone can.'

'He could work a bit faster. Three days now and we're still in my childhood.'

'You must have been a *terrible* little boy. Some of the things I've heard . . .'

Before I could think of a snappy comeback the elevator whooshed to a stop and we emerged at water level. Steps led down into the ocean from an enclosed diving room. The attendant was waiting with our scuba gear ready and we buckled it on and dove in. Straight to the bottom and out among the coral reefs. Even if they came looking they would never find us here. I snapped on the sonar communicator and called in.

'Not much of a search,' the operator told me. 'I'll let you know when they reach the lower level.'

Angelina and I dove deep. Rainbow-hued fish burst out and around us, green plants bowed to our passing. The water was clear and warm and was rapidly restoring my thoughts and good spirits. We swam to a grotto, completely surrounded by coral, that we had found on an earlier visit during an alert, and settled down on the golden sand. I put my arm around Angelina and she snuggled up to me, both for the fun of it and to get our masks touching so we could talk.

'Anything new come in on Kraj and his boys while the doc was slogging through my gray matter?'

'They've been located, but that's all. Now that the first stage of invasion is over the Cliaand forces seem to be settling down for the occupation. They've taken over this immense office building, the Octagon it's called probably because it has eight sides, and have cleared everyone out. They seem to have moved most of their administrative operations there – and one of Kraj's gray men was seen coming out of the building. This must be where they are holed up.'

'I wonder why they left the last building?'

'Afraid of you and your relentless revenge, no doubt.'

I snorted. Hard to do in a face mask. 'You're only saying that, but by Belial there is more than an element of truth in it. The Cliaand operation in general has to be knocked out, but those gray men need special attention. But first we have to grab one of them. I'll have to get inside the building.'

'You'll do nothing of the sort.' She pinched the skin over my ribs and I tried to slap her hand away but you can't do this under water. I settled for a pinch myself, and she was surely far more pinchable than I, and we played around like this for a while until I remembered why she had distracted me and returned ruthlessly to the interrupted conversation.

'Why can't I try to get into the building? I'll be disguised, I speak Cliaandian, I know the ropes . . .'

'And they know yours. They'll have cameras on every entrance feeding data to the computers. Which will know your height, your build, your weight, manner of walk, retinal pattern, the words. You can't disguise everything and you know it. They'll have you in the bag the instant you walk into the place.'

'You're just saying that because it is true,' I muttered. 'So I suppose you have a better plan?'

'I do. I speak Cliaandian and they have no records on me at all. And I'm an experienced field operator, the only one on the planet besides you.'

'No!'

'Why the instant no?' She scowled at me and the next pinch hurt. 'You're my husband, not my owner – remember? I'm as good at this business as you are, maybe better, and there is a job that needs doing. Let's have none of your male superiority and possessiveness.'

She was right of course, but I couldn't let her know it.

'I was only worried about your safety.'

She melted at this, even the smartest woman is a sucker for the loving attention, and rubbed against me. I felt like the heel I was.

'You do love me, Jim, in your own horrible way. But I'll be all right, you'll see. There are some women among the Cliaandian supporting echelons – I don't see how they can wear those ugly uniforms – and the girls and I will grab onto one. With her uniform and identification I'll get into the building, find Kraj—'

'You won't do anything foolish?'

150

'Of course not. This is too important to bungle by trying it alone. I told you I wanted to give him my *personal* attention at my leisure. This will be a scouting trip only. I'll locate the gray men, map the layout and take a look at the detection devices – and leave at once.'

'Great.' I was getting enthusiastic now and trying to put my fears for her safety aside. 'That is all we will need to mount a quick kidnapping. Hit them fast and hard, walk right in and grab Kraj and right out again. Foolproof.'

The sonar communicator buzzed and I flicked it on.

'The search party has gone. You may return.'

We swam back slowly, hand in hand, enjoying the moment. Doctor Mutfak was waiting when we climbed out of the water.

'Good, we pick up where we left off.' There was no warmth at all in his smile. 'The teddy bears, we must probe the symbolism here so we can move on to more recent things.'

He tapped his foot impatiently while Angelina and I clutched in a nice wet embrace and kissed with abandon. Wearing the masks had been quite frustrating. Then back to the room. I let the doctor put me under at once since I didn't want Angelina to catch my jumpiness before she left. The mission would be difficult enough without my giving her things to worry about. She waved and went to dress and I waved back and Mutfak stuck a needle in my arm. No romance in his soul.

We must have moved along nicely because when I awoke next the teddy bears had long since vanished and the last dream I remembered had something to do with exploding spaceships and solar flares. Dr. Mutfak was packing up his instruments and the last glimmer of daylight was fading in the night sky outside.

'Very good,' he said. 'Coming along nicely.'

'Have you uncovered any traces of Kraj's tampering yet?'

'Traces!' His nostrils flared and he puffed out his cheek. 'They are like heavy boot marks all through your cortex! Butchers, those people, simply butchers! Lucky in a way because their traces are so easy to find. Memory blocks all over, traces of amnesia with connections to patterns of false memory. These memories are the only thing of any clinical value and I must find out what techniques they use. They were placed there very quickly, you told me that, yet they are incredibly complete, all senses involved, and detailed as well.'

'I'll vouch for that.'

'I think you will have found them impossible to tell from real memories, that is the strength of their technique. I have removed some major ones that seemed to be disturbing you and in later sessions I will take care of the others. Now – look at your wrists and tell me about the red lines you see there.'

'They look just like red lines,' I said. Then I remembered waking up in the cell and, for some reason believing that my hands had been cut off. I don't know why. They were just red lines.

'A false memory?' I asked.

'Yes, and an outstandingly repulsive one. I'll tell you about it at the next session. But right now you need rest.'

'A fine idea, after I get something to eat . . .'

The door flew open and Taze ran in and, as she passed, I had a quick glimpse of the horrified expression on her face. Sudden fear hit me in the stomach and I sat, watching her, saying nothing while she turned on the TV. The Cliaandians had a propaganda station operating now, though no one bothered to watch it.

The screen lit up and I found myself looking at Kraj. He almost smiled as he spoke.

152

'It's a tape, it keeps repeating,' Taze said.

'. . . that we want him to know. Someone out there must know the man known as James diGriz. Contact him. Tell him to listen to this broadcast. This message is for you, diGriz. We want you back here. I have Angelina here. She is unharmed – as *yet* – and will remain that way until dawn. I suggest you contact me and see me.

'Welcome home, Jim.'

CHAPTER EIGHTEEN

I HAD A NUMBER OF MOMENTS of numb shock after this, during which period I wished to be alone. Taze was understanding enough to leave when I pointed at the exit, but the doctor tried to start a conversation which I terminated by clutching his neck and the seat of his trousers and heaving him through the door which she obligingly held open. Then I kicked in the TV set, an act of wanton destruction that helped a bit, before I poured a stiff cogitating drink. With this in hand I dropped into the chair, looked out unseeingly at the star spread sky, and worked out a plan. This was not going to be simple – and dawn was not that far away.

The thought that kept nibbling at the edge of my awareness was finally faced. I was going to have to surrender and get a collar back on – there was no way of avoiding that. My memories of what that was like were not very nice, in fact my brain sort of twitched a bit inside the bone case at the thought. There had been entirely too much traffic through my gray matter of late and I was not looking forward to any more. Yet it was unavoidable. The collar and torture box had to be part of any plan, and they had to be neutralized. Not a very easy thing to accomplish. I mumbled over all the possibilities and when the attack plan was blocked out I sent for Taze and told her what I was going to do.

'You can't,' she said, and I swear those lovely large eyes were filled with tears, 'turn yourself over to those fiends.

To save a woman. If only the *men* on this planet were like you. Impossible to believe . . .'

I resisted the impulse to enjoy a little warm female solace and turned to snapping open some of the weapon containers. At the sight of the grenades Miss Taze retreated and Sergeant Taze looked on with interest.

'This will be a two part operation,' I told her. 'I'll take care of the first part myself, which will be the penetration of the building and freeing Angelina. I hope to grab a gray man as well, but if that slows me down we'll save that part of the job for another time. The second part of the operation will be getting out of the Octagon, and for that I am going to need your help. I'll need plans of the building, I want to talk to someone who knows his way around it well, someone on the custodial staff if possible, so I can find an area of vulnerability. Can you do this now?'

'At once,' she called back over her shoulder as she left. A reliable girl, our Taze. I dug into the equipment containers.

Dawn was only two hours away before we were ready to move. I had completed my part of the operation, but setting up the escape afterwards wasn't that simple. The Octagon was very much like a fortress in the eyes of the small forces we could muster quickly. And we were hampered by our lack of any aircraft or heavy equipment. There seemed no way out by air or on the ground. It was one of the maintenance staff, finally located and dragged in shivering, who found the exit and pointed it out with a trembling finger on the blueprints.

'Cable tunnel, sir and mam, goes under the street and under the walls and comes up in sub-basement 17. Big tunnel for wires and telephone and that kind of thing.'

'It's sure to be bugged,' I said. 'But if we plan this right it won't matter. Take note, ladies, because I don't want to repeat myself. This is how the operation is going to work.'

155

By the time everything had been taken care of it was less than twenty minutes to dawn and I was in a cold sweat. The first units were moving into position when I put the viewcall in to Kraj. We were connected at once and I talked before he could say anything.

'I want to see Angelina instantly, and talk to her. I have to be absolutely sure she has not been harmed.'

He didn't argue, he had been expecting this. She came into focus and I saw that hated collar with its cable leading up out of the picture.

'Are you all right?'

'As fine as I could possibly be while in the same room with this creature,' she said calmly.

'They've done nothing to you?'

'Nothing as yet, other than to clap this collar around my neck and hook the thing up to the ceiling so I wouldn't run away. But you can imagine the threats this repulsive man has made. I don't think I could live for a moment with a mind like his . . .'

She stiffened then and her eyes rolled up out of sight although her lids didn't close. Kraj had given her a shot of the nerve torture. I knew at that moment that he would never live if I could get my hands on him. His face reappeared on the screen and it took an effort I did not think myself capable of to stare at him calmly and say nothing.

'You'll come to me now, diGriz, and surrender. You only have a few minutes left. You know what will happen to your wife if you don't. If you surrender she will be released at once.'

'What proof do I have that you will keep your word?'

'None whatsoever. But you don't have a choice, do you?'

'I'll be there,' I said as calmly as I could manage and turned the phone off – but not before I heard Angelina's shouted *no* in the background.

'Are those clothes dry yet?' I asked, tearing off my shirt and kicking out of my boots at the same time.

'Just about,' Taze said. She and another girl were holding hot air blowers to a Cliaand uniform that I thought was just right for this occasion. It had been soaked in a chemical bath and was now being force dried.

'Almost is good enough, we can't wait any longer.'

There were some damp patches, but nothing that mattered. We left, and the powerboat was waiting at the hotel dock below, motor rumbling. So far so good. And the car was there on shore with Dr. Mutfak in the back, black bag on his knees, muttering to himself.

'I don't like it,' he said. 'It is really a violation of my medical code of ethics.'

'War is a violation of any code of ethics or morality, a monstrosity against which any weapons must be used. Do what you have been asked.'

'I'll do it, that goes without saying, but a man is allowed to comment upon the ethics involved.'

'Comment. But fill the needle at the same time.'

We parked in a side street, in the darkness, with the Octagon just around the corner.

'Catalyst,' I said, 'and don't spill any. Under my arms where the dampness won't be noticed.

I raised both arms and felt the warmth of the liquid from the insulated container, then quickly lowered my arms to trap the wet fabric between my upper arms and my sides. Then I climbed out of the car and put my hand back in through the window. The needle bit into my flesh and that was that. As I started around the corner I heard the car pull away.

The Octagon loomed up like a mountain before me, the sky beginning to lighten behind it. We had cut this very close. There was an entrance ahead, the one I had been directed to, and two of the gray men were waiting. Both wore gausspistols which were still in the holsters. They were very sure of themselves. I walked up to them silently and one of them clamped a come-along cuff on my wrist and led me in through the doors and past the silent guards. I stumbled going up the stairs and after that looked down carefully to see where I put my feet. The injection was beginning to take effect. There was nothing I wanted to say and my captors, they in their usual fashion, had nothing to say to me. They prodded me in the direction they wanted me to go and pushed me through the doorway of the room they wanted me to enter. Once inside they covered me with their guns while the wrist-cuff was unlocked.

'Clothes off,' one of them ordered.

It was an effort not to smile. There was the fluoroscope off to one side and the other test equipment. These characters were running true to type, following the same routine they had used when I had first been captured. Didn't they realize that routine was a trap and a losing game? No they did not. I fumbled off my clothes and let them work their will upon me.

They found nothing, of course, since there was nothing there to find. Or rather there was one thing that I was sure they would not find. And they didn't. They slowly plodded through their routine examinations and I began to wish they would finish and be done. My head was getting a little foggy from the drug and I felt as though I were wrapped in cotton wool. The injection must be reaching the peak of its effectiveness and would be tapering off soon. What I had to do must be done when the drug was at the height of its power – or close to it – or all the preparations would be useless.

'Put these on,' a wooden faced captor said and threw me the familiar transparent dungarees. I bent to pick them up – and to cover the smile that I could no longer resist. Done it! They did not seem impatient when I fumbled with the closing on the clothes. I had to watch my fingers carefully to be sure they did their job. When the collar locked around my neck I almost heaved a sigh of relief. We were getting close, and the timing was just about perfect. As one of the guards took the torture box and led me out I lowered my head so I could see where I put my feet so I would not stumble. If this generated an illusion of defeat all the better. We went down a wide corridor and past a staircase, and I made a mental note of its location, even counting the paces after it to get some estimate of its distance from our destination.

Which was Kraj's lair. He was waiting behind his desk, as patiently and as emotionlessly as a spider in its web. Angelina sat before him, her torture box hooked to the ceiling.

'Are you all right?' I asked as I came through the door.

'Of course. Nothing has happened. You shouldn't have come.'

As soon as I had this reassurance I turned my attention to Kraj, aware at the same time of the guard closing the door behind us.

'You'll release her now, won't you?' I asked.

'Naturally not. There would be no advantage in that.' His expression never changed while he spoke.

'I didn't think you would. Is there any reason why you shouldn't tell me how you caught her?'

'Your memory contained an exact description of your wife. When we discovered that two women had aided your escape we naturally assumed that one might have been this Angelina. The computer identified her as soon as she entered the building.'

'We were foolish to take the risk,' I said, apparently turning to face her, but looking at the guard instead. He was about to hook my torture box to another hook in the ceiling – and if he did we were trapped.

All I could do was make a dive for him.

'Stop him!' Kraj shouted and the guard looked at me and pressed a quick pattern on the red keys on the box.

I can't pretend that it felt nice. Enough pain leaked through to tear at my stomach with nausea and to knot my muscles. I stumbled and fell at the man's feet, not quite reaching him. The drug I had taken blocked most of the pain, but not all of it. There still had to be nerve pathways open for motor control. My eyes filled with tears and I could not wipe them so my vision blurred and swam. There was a shoe before me and that was no good, and a uniform leg, bad as well.

And then the guard's hand as he bent over to take hold of me. I lashed out with my extended middle finger and scratched the skin on the back of his hand.

He shivered just a bit and kept on bending, almost in slow motion, until he crumpled on the floor next to me, dropping the control box. It was just close enough to reach out and tap the *off* button.

The pain was over, instantly. And Kraj was behind my back. I scrambled and rolled, fighting my knotted muscles, climbing to my feet.

In a few moments since I had attacked the guard the situation had changed drastically. Angelina lay across Kraj's desk, holding on to her collar, writhing in pain. Kraj was on his knees behind the desk reaching for his gun. I dived for him just as he raised it. I was not going to make it, I was too late, he was going to fire and that was that.

But at precisely that moment the distant explosion went off and the floor heaved, dust and bits of plastic shook down from the ceiling and the lights flickered. Kraj had not been expecting this – and I had – and his attention wavered for that vital instant as I slithered across the desk towards him and my fingernail nicked his skin.

He fired, but the slug plowed into the far wall because he was falling, unconscious even as he pulled the trigger.

Angelina must have attacked him as soon as I had dived for the guard. By hanging from the cable she had brought her feet up high enough to get in the one good kick that had sent Kraj over. He had retaliated by going to the radio control before his gun – and this little bit of excess sadism had given me the chance to reach him. But Angelina was paying for this now.

I could not look at her twisting body as I climbed up on the desk beside her. There were a number of controls before Kraj's chair but I was not going to take the time to try to figure them out. Instead I unhooked the box and turned it off. Angelina opened her eyes and lay still, just staring at me as I went through the drawers in the desk.

'Darling, you are a genius,' she said weakly. I found a key and bent to unlock her collar. 'How did you do it?'

'I out-thought them, that's all. They couldn't find any weapons in my clothing because the clothing itself was the weapon. The fabric was soaked in tanturaline which transformed it into a powerful explosive. I put the liquid catalyst on the cloth under my arms where my body heat would keep it from reacting. As long as I was in the uniform nothing happened, but as soon as they made me strip it off – as I was sure they would – the catalyst began to cool and when it reached the critical temperature . . . '

'Boom the whole thing exploded. My genius.' She reached up and pulled me to her as the collar clicked open, and bestowed a warm and passionate kiss that I returned for a bit until I remembered where we were and disentangled gently. She sat up shakily and tried the key in my collar.

'And I suppose you have some wonderfully ingenious explanation of how you killed these fiends?'

'Not dead yet, just unconscious. I filed one fingernail to a point sharp enough to scratch skin, then painted it with callanite.'

'Of course! Invisible to the eye and it would take a spectometric test to find the tiny trace. But more than enough to render the scratchee instantly unconscious. What next?'

'A phone call to get the rest of the operation going in case that explosion wasn't heard outside of the building. But they have listening devices . . . '

Before I could finish the sentence the lights went out. Since the room had no windows we were in complete darkness and I was lost, falling, out of contact with reality.

'Angelina!' I called out, aware of the hoarseness of my voice. 'I am juiced to the eyeballs with narco drugs that cut off almost all pain sensation, which is why I could polish off the guard even though he was jazzing me with his shock box. But this also means I can't feel anything at all – I'm completely numb. All I can do is hear in the darkness. You'll have to help.'

'What should I do?'

'Find Kraj and drag him over to me. I'm going to see if we can't get him out with us.'

She pulled him out from behind the desk, none too gently from the sounds I heard, and helped me get him up on my shoulders.

'Now lead us out of here. You'll have to guide me because I have no way at all of moving around in this darkness. Across to the other side of the hall, then left for about 45 meters until you come to the stairs. Then down, all the way.'

Angelina took my hand and we were off. I slammed into a couple of things but that wasn't her fault since

I still had no sense of touch. It was easier and faster in the hall where she could follow the wall with one hand. There were voices shouting in the distance as well as one or two satisfying screams. My exploding wardrobe was providing plenty of distraction, coupled with the electrical failure. Then, just as I was congratulating myself on how well things were going, the lights flickered and came back on dimly.

We stopped, frozen, blinking in the sudden illumination and feeling as though we were in the middle of a spot-lit stage. There must have been at least a dozen people in sight.

But they were all ignoring us, involved in their own troubles, barely aware of each other. A uniformed fat official actually ran by us, eyes wide with fear after the explosion and the darkness, not even seeing us.

'The stairway, quick,' I said and lumbered forward as fast as I could with Kraj bounding on my shoulders.

Of course it was too good to last. The emergency lights flickered and dimmed redly and seemed about to expire at any minute. A soldier coming towards us had enough time to look and to think about what he was see-ing. It finally dawned on him that something was wrong and he raised his gaussrifle and shouted to us to stop.

Angelina had Kraj's pistol and she fired just once. The soldier folded and we were at the stairs – when the lights went out again and stayed out.

The stairs were difficult to maneuver, though some sensation was coming back and I could feel a certain amount. But I dropped Kraj once, we both laughed a little at this and rolled him down an extra step or two for good measure, and a moment later I fell against Angelina and almost toppled us both headlong. After this we went more carefully and one flight down someone spoke.

'We've been waiting to take you out. Just stand still.'

It was a girl's voice, and not speaking Cliaandian, or Angelina would have blown the whole stair well up. We waited and I felt someone's hands touching my head, putting on a pair of heavy glasses. Then I could see again, with everything in harsh contrast. They were infrared goggles and the girl who was waiting for us had a hand projector. We went down almost at a run after that, while she called on her comradio. Taze was waiting at the foot of the stairs.

'We sent people up all the staircases to try and contact you. They are coming back now. This way.'

They took Kraj from me. I couldn't feel any pain or fatigue, but I was sure from the way my muscles were vibrating that I would ache all over when the drug wore off. We went at a fast trot to the open mouth of the service tunnel.

'In,' Taze ordered. 'There are cars waiting at the other end.'

CHAPTER NINETEEN

WHENEVER I MOVED I groaned. A little more hollowly and theatrically than was really called for by my condition, but it made Angelina feel wanted and took her mind off her troubles. She clucked about like a mother hen, plumping the pillows under my head, pouring me soothing drinks, peeling sweet fruits and cutting them into tiny pieces for me to nibble on. I hoped that these wifely ministrations would keep her from remembering the torture box of the day before, and if she were thinking about this she never mentioned it. The air that moved in through the open windows was warm and the sky its usual brilliant blue.

'Were there any casualties?' I said. 'I meant to ask when I woke up but my head is still swimming in slow circles.'

'None to speak of. Some burns and scrapes and a few superficial wounds among the rear guard. Apparently everything went off just as you had planned. As soon as the explosion was heard they shorted all the phone and power lines that led to the Octagon and made a fearful mess of the wiring. Then the girls came through the tunnel and knocked out the emergency generator. You know the rest since you were obliging enough not to keel over until we reached the cars.'

'I would have been happy to do it earlier but I did not relish the thought of being dragged through the pipes by Taze's amazons. They still don't seem to think much of men. Maybe they'll make me an honorary girl.'

'Let's see that is all they make you. Dr. Mutfak phoned

a little while ago to say that he had Kraj almost to the point where we could talk to him.'

'Then let's go. This is a conversation I have been looking forward to for a long time.'

When I got out of the bed my muscles creaked and snapped and I felt a thousand years old. I was wearing swimming attire, as was Angelina; informality was the order of the day at the luxurious Ringa Baligi. This also enabled us to do our dive for life if any troops came nosing around. Which made me think.

'What happens if any interfering Cliaandians come this way? I assume plans have been made to hide Kraj.'

'Hide is the correct word. Since he is unconscious he can be stowed in the back of one of the refrigerators. A good idea, particularly if they forget and leave him there.'

'Vengeance later, information now. I wonder what fascinating facts the good doctor has uncovered about our alien?'

'He is not an alien,' Dr. Mutfak insisted. While I slept he had been working in the small but complete laboratory that was part of the mini-hospital in the hotel. 'I will stake my reputation on it.'

'The only reputation that you have that I know of is as a brain-squeezer,' I said. 'Can you be sure . . . '

'I will not be insulted by foreigners!' the doctor shouted, drawing himself up in anger so the top of his head almost reached my shoulder. 'Insults from females I am used to, but from offworlders I will not bear. Even on the nameless planet where you were spawned it must be known that the basis of all medical training is a sound grounding in biology and physiology. It so happens that cytology is a bit of a hobby of mine – I could show you cells that would have you crying aloud with wonder – so I know what I am about. This man's cells are human, so he is human. A viable homo sapiens.'

'But the differences, so alien, his low body temperature, the lack of emotions, all that.'

'All well within the realm of human variation. Mankind is quite adaptable, and generations of survival in various environments produce suitable adaptations. There are many more exotic instances cited in the literature than are represented by this individual.'

'Then he couldn't be a robot either?' Angelina asked with wide-eyed innocence, skittering away when I reached to grab her. My theories didn't seem to be holding up too well.

'When can we talk to him?' I asked.

'Soon, soon.'

'Is it permitted to ask what you have done to him that will make him amenable to questioning?'

'A good question.' Mutfak fingered his silvery beard and concentrated on interpreting the mysteries of medicine for the layman.

'Since this is the man who appears to be responsible for the major and harmful tampering with your brain I did not feel what might be called the usual moral responsibility of doctor to patient, particularly when the patient has helped arrange the ruthless invasion of my planet as well.'

'Good for you, Doc.'

'Therefore I have been quite single-minded and have circumvented his normal thought processes for our benefit and not for his. I did not do this easily, and feel it is just as much a moral crime as what was done to you, but I will take the responsibilities of the act. The fact that he was unconscious when brought here was a help. I have planted false memories and caused regression in areas of attitude and emotions, put in memory blocks and in general have done some terrible things for which I will carry shame until the day I die.'

167

Dr. Mutfak looked as though he might cry at any moment and I patted him on the shoulder.

'You're a front line soldier, Doctor, going into battle. Doing what you have to do to win. We all respect you for it.'

'Well I don't, but I shall worry about that later.' He shook himself and was the man of science again. 'In a few minutes I shall bring the patient up from the deep trance. He will appear to be awake but his conscious mind will have little or no awareness of what is happening. His emotional attitudes will be those of a child of about age two who wants help. Remember that. Do not force questions or act hostile. He wants to aid you in every way he can, but many times won't have access to the information easily. Be kind and rephrase the question. Don't push too hard. Are you ready?'

'I guess so.' Though I found it hard to think of Kraj as a cooperative kiddy.

Angelina and I trooped along behind the doctor, into the dimly lit hospital room. A male nurse who had been sitting by the bed stood up when we came in. Mutfak arranged the lighting so most of it fell on Kraj while we sat in half darkness, then gave the man an injection.

'This should work quite fast,' he said.

Kraj's eyes were closed, his face slack and unmoving. White bandages wrapped his skull and a handful of wires slipped out from under them to the machines beside the bed.

'Wake up, Kraj, wake up,' the doctor said.

Kraj's face stirred, his cheek twitched and his eyes slowly opened. His expression was one of calm serenity and there was a trace of a shy smile on his lips.

'What is your name?'

'Kraj.' He spoke softly in a hoarse voice that reminded me of a young boy's. There were no traces of resistance.

'Where do you come from?'

He frowned, blinking at me, and stammered some meaningless sounds. Angelina leaned forward and patted his hand and spoke in a friendly tone.

'You must be calm, don't rush. You have come here from Cliaand, haven't you?'

'That's right.' He nodded and smiled.

'Now think back, you have a good memory. Were you born on Cliaand?'

'I – I don't think so. I have been there a long time, but I wasn't born there. I was born at home.'

'Home is another world, a different planet?'

'That's right.'

'Could you tell me what it is like at home?'

'Cold.'

When he said it his voice was as chill as the word, more like the Kraj we knew, and his face worked constantly, expressions echoing his words.

'Always cold. Nothing green, nothing grows, the cold doesn't stop. You have to like cold and I never did though I can live with it. There are warm worlds and many of us go to them. But there are not many of us. We don't see each other very much, I don't think we like each other and why should we? There is nothing to like about snow and ice and cold. We fish, that is all, nothing lives on the snow. All the life is in the sea. I put my arm in once but I could not live in the water. They do and we eat them. There are warmer worlds.'

'Like Cliaand?' I asked, quietly as Angelina had done. He smiled.

'Like Cliaand. Warm all the time, hot too, too hot, but I don't mind that. Strange to see living things on the land other than people. There is a lot of green.'

'What is the name of home, of the cold world?' I whispered.

'The name . . . the name . . . '

The transformation was immediate. Kraj began to writhe on the bed, his face twisted and working, his eyes wide and staring. Dr. Mutfak was shouting at him to forget the question, to lie still, while he tried to get a hypodermic needle into his thrashing arm. But it was too late. The reaction I had triggered went on and, just for an instant, I swear there was the light of intelligence and hatred in his eyes as the conscious Kraj became aware of what was happening.

But only for that moment. An instant later his back arched in a silent spasm and he collapsed, still and unmoving.

'Dead,' Dr. Mutfak pronounced, looking at his telltale instruments.

'That was useful,' Angelina said, walking to the window and throwing open the curtains. 'Time for a swim if you feel up to it, darling. Then we'll have to think of a way to get another gray man for Dr. Mutfak. Now that we know the area to avoid we can make him last longer while he is questioned.'

The doctor recoiled. 'I couldn't, not again. We killed him, I killed him. There was an implanted order, an irresistible order, to die rather than reveal where this planet is. It can be done, the death wish. I have seen it now. Never again.'

'We have been raised differently, doctor,' Angelina said, calmly and without passion. 'I would shoot a creature like Kraj in battle and I feel no differently about his dying in this manner. You know what he is and what he has done.'

I said nothing because I agreed with them both. Angelina who saw the galaxy as a jungle, survival as a matter of eating or being eaten. And the doctor, a humanitarian who had been raised in a matriarchy, stable and unchanging, peaceful and at peace. They were both right. An interesting animal is man.

'Take a rest, Doc,' I said. 'Take one of your own pills. You have been up for a day and a night and that can't be doing you any good. We'll see you when you wake up, but have a good rest first.'

I took Angelina's arm and guided her out, away from the sad little man who was staring, unseeing, at the floor.

'You don't feel sorry for that Kraj creature?' Angelina asked, giving me her number two frown which means something like I'm not looking for trouble, but if you are you are certainly going to get it.

'Me? Not much chance, love. Kraj is the man who unreeled the barbed wire in my brain a while back and tried to do the same to you. I'm only sorry we couldn't get more from him before he left us.'

'The next one will tell more. At least we know now that your idea was right. They may not be aliens, but they certainly aren't natives of Cliaand. If we can root them out of there we might be able to stop the entire invasion thing.'

'Easier visualized than accomplished. Let's have that swim and brood about it over a drink when we come out.'

The water loosened up my muscles and made me profoundly aware of a great hunger and thirst. I called in on my sonar communicator so that a small steak and a bottle of beer were waiting at the water's edge when we emerged. These barely brushed the fringes of my appetite yet gave me the strength to make it back to our room for a more elaborate meal.

And elaborate it was, seven courses beginning with a fiery Burada soup, going on to fish and meat and other delicacies too numerous to mention. Angelina ate a bit then sipped at her wine while I finished most of the food in sight. Finally replete I ordered the soiled dishes away and settled back with a sigh.

'I have been thinking,' I said.

'You could have fooled me. I thought you were eating like a pig with both trotters in the trough.'

'Just save the bucolic humor. A hard night's work deserves a good day's food. Cliaand, that's our problem. Or rather the gray men who have her war economy so firmly under control. I'll bet if we could get rid of them the original Cliaandians would not have this same burning interest in interstellar conquest.'

'Simple enough. A program of planned assassination. There can't be too many of them, Kraj said as much. Polish them off. I'll be glad to take on the assignment.'

'Oh no you won't. No wife of mine hires out as a contract gun. It is not that simple – physically or morally. The gray men can guard themselves well. And that the ends justify the means is a bankrupt statement. You saw what happened to Dr. Mutfak when he worked for a good end but used means that ran counter to his moral beliefs. You and I are of tougher fabric, my love, but we would still be affected if we went in for mass slaughter . . . '

She went white and I was sorry I had said it. I took her hand.

'I didn't mean it that way. I wasn't talking about the past.'

'I know, but it still stirred up some unwholesome memories. Let's forget assassination. What else can be done?'

'A number of things, I am sure, if we can only ask just the right questions. There must be a way to break apart the constantly expanding Cliaand empire.'

Angelina touched the wine glass to her lips and a highly attractive concentration line appeared between her eyes.

172

'What about starting counter-revolutions or rebellions on all the conquered worlds?' she said. 'If we kept the Cliaandians busy fighting on the presently conquered planets they couldn't very well go seeking for new territory.'

'You're nibbling close to the idea there, but it's not quite right yet. We can't expect much from the resistance movements on these different worlds if the example of Burada is at all relevant. You heard what Taze said, the fighting is dying down because of the massive reaction by the Cliaand forces. If one of them is killed in a raid they slaughter twenty Buradans in return. These people, after generations of peace are not mentally equipped to fight a ruthless guerrilla war. I even doubt if the Cliaandians would react so viciously if they weren't forced on by the gray men who organized and order everything. The soldiers just follow orders, and following orders has always been a Cliaand strength. We'll never stop these people by trying to incite minor revolts behind their backs. But you are right about causing them trouble on the various worlds. The entire Cliaandian economy and culture is set up on a continuing wartime basis. It is like some demented life form that must keep expanding or die. Cliaand itself can't possibly build or supply its fleets but must depend on the conquered worlds. These worlds are in the absolute control of the Cliaand so they take orders and turn out the goods and the invasions roll on and nothing can stop the advance.'

'I wish the Cliaand invasion was that demented life form you talk about, some sort of ugly green growing thing. We could tear it up by the roots, break off the limbs—' She broke a hard roll in half to demonstrate what she meant, then nibbled at it. When she started to speak again I held up my hand.

173

'Stop,' I ordered. 'Say nothing. I think. I see something. It is almost there.'

Then I paced the room, putting two and two together and getting four and adding four and getting eight and performing equally skilled problems of mathematics and logic. It was clear, all clear, and the pieces fell into place and I fell into my chair and grabbed up my drink.

'I am a genius,' I said.

'I know. That's why I married you. Physically you are very unattractive.'

'You will soon be apologizing for that remark, woman. For the moment we will drink to my Plan and to victory.'

We clinked and sipped.

'What plan?' she asked.

'I cannot tell you yet. Aside from the fact that you scoffed, it is not detailed in all its ramifications and must be worked out. But the first step is clear and will begin at once or sooner. Do you think the gray men have made a public announcement of Kraj's kidnapping?'

'I doubt it. We've heard nothing on the command circuits we monitor. And I'm sure this is not the kind of news they would want the Cliaandian man-in-the-spaceship to know about.'

'Just my thinking. Add to this the exaggerated aloofness and self-centered attitude that they have, even towards each other. I am going to gamble on the fact that there has been no widespread announcement about Kraj.'

'How?'

'Get the makeup and facelifting kit. I am going to get into the military base disguised as Kraj. I have some important things to do there.'

She started to protest, but I raised my finger and she was silent. Just as I had been when she went to the Octagon. There was nothing she could say and she knew it.

Without a word she went for the disguise materials.

CHAPTER TWENTY

I NEEDED CLIAANDIAN TRANSPORTATION and I got it in the simplest way possible. From the enemy. Since I wasn't outrageously happy about the makeup job we had done I decided to operate after dark when the dim lights would help the illusion. Then, wearing Kraj's uniform and carrying my own case, I went with Hamal to the Octagon, scene of the earlier festivities. Hamal was a member of the auxiliary police, male that is, since the women made up most of the force. I would have preferred one of the girls, they seemed much more sure of themselves, but there were only male Cliaand troops on the planet at this time. The handful of Cliaand women stayed out of sight. Hamal looked a little nervous and I didn't like the way he rolled his eyes from time to time, but he would have to do.

'You understand your part?' I asked him, pushing him into the shadowed entrance to the deep doorway.

'I do, sir, sure I do.'

Were his teeth chattering? It was hard to tell. I took out the vial Dr. Mutfak had given me for use in case of emergency.

'Take two of these, chew and swallow. They're happy pills that should raise your morale without sending you dancing through the streets.'

'I don't . . .'

'You do now. Take.'

He took and I scuttled away towards the Octagon, keeping to the shadows, and looking carefully around the corner before I made my play. There was a certain amount of traffic in and out of the building even at this hour of the night, but nothing that would help me. Finally a small ground car pulled up and dropped two officers off, then started away. In my direction. All systems go. I stepped into the street in front of it and waved my hand; it squealed to a stop with the front bumper almost touching me. The driver looked frightened and I kept him that way.

'Do you always drive like that?'

'No, sir, but . . . '

'Save your excuses, they don't interest me.' I climbed into the car next to him while he was still gaping. 'Drive on, I'll tell you where I want to go.'

'Sir, this car, I mean . . . '

A single, cold, Krajian look wilted him like a spring flower in a blizzard and he shot the car forward. As soon as we were out of sight of the building I ordered him to stop and broke a sleep capsule under his nose. I'm sure he could use the rest. Then I drove him to the place where Hamal was waiting. He had pried open the door to the stationery store in which he was hiding, and we carried the Cliaand trooper inside. He would sleep until morning after that capsule and I arranged reams of paper comfortably under his head and feet while Hamal changed into his uniform.

'Do you know how to drive this car?' I asked him when we emerged.

'I should. It's one of ours. They stole it and painted their dirty flag on it.'

'Spoils of war regained. Now drive me to the spaceport. And don't stop completely at the gate, just slow down and keep rolling. It's all bluff so keep your chin up and try not to look as scared as you are. Be a man.'

'I am,' he moaned. 'But this is a woman's job. I don't know how I ever got myself talked into it.'

'Shut up and drive on. And take a couple more of these pills.'

The spaceport was ahead and I was more worried about my driver than I was about anyone there. I had seen the way they stayed out of Kraj's way. Perhaps that would help to explain my driver's obvious fear. I sighed. Roll on the car. Everyone was supposed to know Kraj – and now I was putting that theory to the test. The guards snapped to attention when we appeared and the sergeant started to say something, but I talked first.

'Stay away from that phone. I want to talk to some people and I don't want you telling them I'm coming. You know what will happen to you if you do.' I had to shout the last words since, in his near panic, Hamal had not slowed enough and we zipped right by the guards. But they must have heard because they made no attempt that I could see to get near their phone. Step one.

'I can't do it!' Hamal sobbed and spun the wheel on the car until we were headed back towards the gate. 'I'm going home. I was never cut out for the police, it was all my mother's idea, she wanted me to be like a daughter to her and made a tomgirl out of me. When all I ever wanted to be was a simple househusband like my father . . . '

The gate was coming up at a great rate and I cursed fluently and jumbled out a sleep capsule to crack in front of his face, then tugged at the wheel. I had to hold him up with the other hand and we made another turn and zipped off into the night again. I hesitated to think what the guards at the gate thought about all this. Struggling with the controls I managed to guide the car to the rear of one of the big hangars before Hamal's foot slipped off the accelerator and the engine died.

There were crates of some kind in the rear of the car as well as a bundle of army blankets. I heaved everything out except the blankets which I used to cover Hamal, now curled up sweetly on the floor. Perhaps I should have shot him or just dumped him out. But it really wasn't his fault that he was born low man in a matriarchy. As long as no one came near the car we were safe, and I did not feel that anyone would show that much interest in Kraj's car. I drove to the nearest spacer, a great cargo transport, and parked well away from the lights around the entrance. Now for step two.

'You know who I am?' I said to the master at arms stationed at the foot of the gangway. My voice cold and empty.

'Yes, sir, I do.' He stood at attention staring directly ahead of him.

'All right, then have the Chief Engineer meet me on A deck.'

'He's not aboard, sir.'

'I've made a note of that dereliction of duty and you will tell him of it when he returns. His assistant then.'

I went by him without a further look and he sprang to the telephone. By the time I had reached A deck an engineer in greasy coveralls was waiting for me, nervously wiping his hands on a cloth.

'I'm sorry, we were taking down one of the generators . . . ' his voice ran out and expired as I glared at him.

'I know you have trouble, and that is why I am here. Take me to the engine room.'

He hurried away and I followed heavily after him. This was going to be easier than I thought. Three white-faced ratings looked up from the guts of the generator when we came in.

178

'Get them out of here,' I said and did not have to repeat myself.

I looked at the open generator and nodded sagely as if I had any idea what the repairs were about. Then I began a slow tour of the engine room, tapping dials and squinting into observation ports while the engineer trotted after me. When I reached the warpdrive generator I looked at the nameplate covered with incomprehensible numbers and then turned to the engineer.

'Why is this model being used?'

I have never seen an engineer yet who didn't have something to say about every piece of equipment under his care and this one was no different.

'We know it is the older model, sir, but the replacement didn't arrive in time to install and balance before the flight.'

'Bring me the tech manual.'

As soon as his back was turned I squeezed the handle of my case and the bomb dropped into my hand. I set the delay for forty minutes, armed it, and activated the sticky molecules on the base. Then I bent down and pushed it up under the thick housing of the warpdrive generator where it could not be seen. I was examining another piece of equipment by the time the engineer returned with the manual. A quick flip through the pages and a grunt or two over the identification numbers satisfied him, and I handed it back. I felt ashamed because the job was so easy.

'See that the work is done quickly,' I said as I left, specifying nothing, but receiving in return his fervent assurances that it would be so.

I repeated this maneuver at the next spacer, parking my car in the shadows near it. Just about the time I realized that there was something familiar about the ship Ostrov came down the gangway and turned to face me.

This sudden confrontation startled me as much as it did him. But his eyes bulged and he stopped dead while I, being deep in the Kraj role, only stared coldly at him. Would he recognise me? I had bunked with him and drunk with him during my Vaska Hulja days, and I had piloted this ship. The Kraj disguise was good – but could it be expected to stand up to this close examination by someone who knew me so well?

'Well?' I whispered finally, when he showed no intention of moving or speaking or doing anything other than stare.

'I'm sorry, sir, you surprised me. I didn't expect to see you here, if you know what I mean.' He began to sweat and I stayed silent. 'Your voice,' he said finally. 'Is there anything wrong?'

Of course there was. I knew I couldn't make my voice sound like the real Kraj's to someone who had talked with him recently as Ostrov had. I also knew that one whisper sounds very much like any other whisper. But I wasn't telling him that.

'A wound,' I husked. 'After all there is a war on – and some of us are fighting it.'

'Yes, of course, I understand.'

He jittered back and forth from one foot to the other and I had enough of this and pushed on by. But he called after me and I turned with cold impatience to face him again.

'I'm sorry to bother you. I was just wondering if you have heard anything about the whereabouts of Vaska . . .'

'That is not his name. He is a spy. You aren't trying to become familiar with a spy, are you?' Ostrov flushed red, but went on.

'No, of course not, spy, that's what he is. But we were friends once, he wasn't a bad sort then. I was just inquiring.'

'I'll do the inquiring, you do the piloting.'

I turned after these appropriately Krajian words and stamped into the ship. Ostrov had surprised me standing up to Kraj like that. Somewhere inside his alcoholic hide there was a human being struggling for release.

This bomb was as easy to plant as the first one had been and I set it to go off at roughly the same time. Working fast now I drove quickly from ship to ship and managed to plant seven more bombs before the first one went boom. I was in engine room number nine when the alarm sounded.

'What is that?' I asked, hearing the distant moan of sirens.

'I have no idea,' the elderly engineer said, and pointed back to the engines. 'These liner tubes, second rate and shoddy and I can't get replacements . . .'

'I'm no supply officer,' I snarled, suddenly very much in a hurry. 'Go find out what the trouble is.'

As soon as he left I slipped the bomb into place, set it for three minutes and followed him out.

'What is it?' I asked, meeting him at the top of the gangway.

'An explosion in one of the ships, in the engineroom.'

'Where? I must look into this!'

I shouted the words and exited as fast as I could. Almost all of the bombs should have gone off by now and the reports would be pouring in. At first it would all be confusion, and it was during this period that I had to make my exit from the base. Because soon after that would come the realization that all of the explosions had occurred in the same place in a number of ships, followed by the unbelievable news that Kraj had recently been in all of these enginerooms. Kraj would not be suspected, not at first, but the authorities would certainly like to have a little chat with him. I wanted to get out before this final stage was reached. Walking as fast as I could without attracting attention, I headed for my car.

And saw the two military policemen standing there, holding the sagging Hamal between them.

'Is this your car, sir?' one of them asked.

'Of course. What are you doing here?'

'It's this man, we saw him sitting in the back talking to himself. We thought he was drunk until we heard him speak. Some foreign language, sir, sounds like the one they talk on this planet. Do you know who he is?'

I didn't hesitate. This was war and troops die for a lot of reasons.

'Never saw him before in my life.'

My voice penetrated Hamal's drugged brain because he looked up, blinking. Weak as his nerve was, he must have the physical constitution of an ox to be even moving after the amount of gas he had breathed. Then he groped for me shouting aloud.

'You must help me, they are going to kill me, get me out of here, it was a mistake bringing me in the first place . . .'

'What's he saying?' one of the military policemen asked.

'I have no idea – though I think he might be the spy who has been causing the engineroom sabotage.' Time was going by too quickly; how soon before they thought of Kraj? 'Put him in the back of the car and come with me. I know how to make him talk sense.'

While they were doing this I started the engines and pulled away, even before they sat down. This tumbled them about a bit and if they noticed the blankets on the floor they did not mention them. Throttle wide open I headed for the exit.

Towards the officer who stood blocking the way, holding up his hand for me to stop. I kept going but had to brake hard at the last instant because he did not move.

'You cannot leave. The base is closed.' He was coldeyed, hard-faced and mean. So was I.

'I am leaving. Save your orders for others.'

'My orders were to close the gate to *everyone* without exception.'

'I have a prisoner who may be a saboteur and I have two men to guard him. I am taking him to the Octagon for questioning. Your professional zeal is commendable, Captain, but you must know that I am the one who issues orders, not obeys them.'

'You cannot leave.'

Either he was bullheaded to an insane degree – or he had specific orders about me. I had not time to find out. Through the window I could see one of the men answering the phone and I had a sharp suspicion what that call might be. I drew my pistol and pointed it at the captain.

'Move or I will kill you,' I said, in as bored a monotone as I could manage.

He half reached for his gun – then stopped. For a moment more he hesitated and I could see the worried fear in his eyes. Then he stepped aside reluctantly and I gunned the car forward. I had a brief glimpse of a soldier running out of the guardhouse, pointing at the car, shouting something that was drowned in the roar of the engine. After that I did not look back, though the military policemen obviously did. In the rear view mirror I saw them whispering together and they might have been reaching for their guns. I took no chances. As soon as we turned the first corner I threw a gas grenade into the back seat, then stopped just long enough to unload my brace of sleeping beauties.

Hamal was also now very soundly asleep and I strongly wished that I were as well. I yawned broadly and, following the side roads, headed for the dock.

CHAPTER TWENTY-ONE

'Explain, diGriz, explain and make it good.'

Inskipp was in his usual charming humor, growling and snarling and pacing the length of the spacer's lounge.

'First tell me how the children are, my sons, never seen by their father, how do they do?'

'Yes, how are they?' Angelina asked, sitting back comfortably in one of the lounge chairs. Inskipp spluttered a bit but had to answer.

'Doing fine. Putting on weight. Eat a lot just like their father. You'll see them soon. Now enough of that. I come I don't know how many light years to supervise this operation because it seems to have ground to a full stop. And what do I find? My two agents have had enough and have deserted the planet of their assignment and meet me here in orbit – even though said planet is clamped beneath the iron heel of the Cliaand. Explain.'

'We have won.'

'No jokes, diGriz. I can have you shot.'

'You won't hurt me, you have too much invested in my hide. And I meant what I said. We have won. Burada, clamped under the iron heel, doesn't know it yet. The Cliaandian clampers don't know it yet. Just the privileged few.'

'I'm not one of that happy number. Talk faster.'

'A demonstration is in order. Angelina my sweet, do you have our little toy?'

She opened a box next to her chair and handed over the Thing. It was smooth and black and no bigger than my hand. There were small openings on its bottom and at each end, while one end had a cluster of tiny lenses as well. I held it out to Inskipp who looked at it suspiciously.

'Do you know what this is?' I said.

'No. And I can't say that I really care to.'

'This is the tombstone on the grave of all the Cliaandian expansionist ambitions. What type of space vessel is this we are aboard?'

'A light destroyer, Gnasher class. And what relevancy does that have?'

'Patience, and all will be revealed.'

I next took the small control box from Angelina and inserted the end of the spiked rod projecting from it into the matched opening in the Thing. Then I tapped out the serial number for Gnasher class destroyers on the keyboard. With the control box still attached I carried the Thing to the lounge exit where we could see the bulky disc of the main airlock. Angelina followed, leading the protesting Inskipp.

'We must imagine,' I said, 'that this ship is on the ground and that the lock is open. All airlocks open sooner or later and when they do the Thing is waiting. And so is the operator, watching from up to three kilometers away. The lock opens and he activates the Thing. It soars straight at the open lock, through it, and—'

I pressed the *go* button and it went. Tiny jets screamed and it darted off like an impassioned hummingbird, down the hallway towards the stern.

'After it!' I shouted and led the way at a dead run.

We caught up with it two decks down where it had been stopped by a closed door – but not stopped for long. The thermal lance in the Thing's nose burned a quick hole through the metal and it was off again. When we reached the engineroom it had almost eaten its way through this thicker door and there was just time to throw the door open as it went through. It zoomed once around the room as though getting its bearings, so small and fast it was almost impossible to follow, then it dived.

Right at the warpdrive generator where it exploded in a puff of black smoke.

'A harmless smoke charge,' I said. 'To be replaced in field operation by high explosive, more than enough to destroy the warpdrive generator, yet small enough not to cause any other damage. A humane weapon indeed.'

'You're mad.'

'Only at the Cliaand and the gray men for pursuing this futile war. If we can go back for that drink now I'll tell you how it is going to be stopped.'

Comfortably seated, throat cooled, I explained.

'I personally polished off the warpdrive generators in nine of the Cliaand ships, just to see if it could be done and if there would be any unusual problems in ship design or construction. There were none. Cliaandian ships are just like any other ships, only more so since they like a good deal of uniformity which makes our job that much easier. The Thing has been designed to do that job. The Thing operator can sit at his ease outside of a spaceport, watching the Cliaand ships through high powered glasses. When the observed ship opens its port the Thing strikes. The operator must merely aim it, feed in the type of ship, and start it on its way. The Thing has a molecular level memory bank and computer circuitry. It zeroes in on the ship at high speed, finds the port and enters and then, using its programmed knowledge of the vessel's interior, it makes its way to the engine room, stopping for nothing. Where it blows up the warpdrive generator. End of the Cliaand invasion.'

'End of one warpdrive generator,' Inskipp said, a sneer in his voice. 'They order up another one and that is that.'

'That is not that. Generators are complex and not easy

186

to build. There are very few factories that turn them out because most people are satisfied to buy them from someone else. I am sure the Cliaand have at least one factory, but that can be found and knocked out from space.'

'So they get one from the warehouse.'

'There is a limit to the number they can have, and quite soon the warehouse will be empty. Because we are going to have agents on every planet now ruled by the Cliaand and they are going to blow up every warpdrive generator on every ship on those planets. We won't have to go anywhere near the home planet. The warpdrive will be knocked out of cargo ships, war ships, any and all within the Cliaand area of control. Nor will they be able to get any from the outside since this is one embargo that it will be easy for the corps and the cooperating planets to enforce. End of an empire.'

'How?'

'Think, Inskipp, age couldn't have withered your brain as much as your leathery hide. Angelina gave me the clue. The Cliaandians must keep expanding or perish. They don't have enough food on their single planet to carry on this kind of continual expansion. So they conquer a planet, put it to work on their behalf, then restored and resupplied go on to bigger and better things. Only not any more. They still have their planets and the materials – but what good are they if they can't be transported to where they are needed? The expansion will have to stop, and as the ships grow scarce they will have to pull back. Further and further back until they are on their home planet again and that will be the end of that. Any single planet can support itself with raw materials and food, at least enough to survive. But an empire cannot survive with its trade arteries cut. I give them a year, no more, before Cliaand is just another backwater planet with a lot of guys in uniforms and out of jobs. When it is all over normal trade can be started again. A year at the outside. What do you think?'

'I think you did it again, my boy, as I knew you would.'

He beamed at me and I winked at Angelina and we drank to that.

CHAPTER TWENTY-TWO

WE WERE STANDING AT THE INNER LOCK, ready to disembark from the spaceship, when one of the pursers hurried over and handed me a psigram. Angelina blasted it with a withering look.

'Tear it up,' she said. 'If that is from foul Inskipp canceling the one little vacation we have ever had . . .'

'Relax,' I said, glancing through it quickly. 'Our holiday is still safe. This is from Taze . . .'

'If that topheavy hussy is still chasing you she is in for trouble.'

'Have no fear, my love. The communication is of a political nature. The results of the first election to be held since the Cliaandian withdrawal are in. The men's Konsolosluk party have been swept from office and the girls are back at the helm. Taze has been appointed Minister of War, so I don't think future invasion will be as easy as the last. The psigram further states that we have both been awarded the Order of the Blue Mountains, First Class, and there will be much ceremony and medal pinning when next we get to Burada.'

'Just see you don't try going there on your own, Slippery Jim.'

I sighed as the massive outer lock of the spaceship ground open and the militant oompah of band music was carried in by the outside air. The sky was clear and empty of anything other than the puffy white clouds and a copter towing a banner that read WELCOME WELCOME.

'Very nice,' I said.

189

'Urgh urgh,' Bolivar said, or something like that, or was it James who had spoken? They were hard to tell apart and Angelina took a very antipathetic view towards my suggestion that we paint a B on one little forehead and J on the other. Just for awhile. She bent over their tiny forms in the robopram, tucking in blankets and doing other unessential maternal things. Only I knew that she had a gun in her girdle and a knife in the nappies. My Angelina is just as motherly as any female tiger: she takes care of her cubs but also keeps her claws sharp just in case. Pity the poor kidnapper who tried to swipe the diGriz babies!

'That's an improvement over the usual rattling escalator,' I said, pointing to the platform outside.

A shipyard repair stage had been polished and decorated with flags and turned into a passenger elevator. It not only held all the people disembarking but there was plenty of room left over for the military band. Who were now thumping and trumpeting and generally having a good time. We strolled out onto the platform and the robopram rolled after us. James – or was it Bolivar? – tried to hurl himself out of it but a padded tentacle pushed him back to the pillows.

'It doesn't look so bad,' Angelina said, looking out across the spaceport to the city while the stage slowly descended. 'I can't understand what you were complaining about.'

'Let's say the reception was a bit different last time I was here. Isn't that a pleasant sight?'

I pointed to the row upon row of abandoned spaceships, the streaks of rust on their sides visible even from here.

'Very nice,' she said, not looking, tucking in an infant that the robopram had already done an excellent job on. Like all new fathers I was more than a little jealous of the attention lavished on the kiddies, and I looked forward to the new joint assignment when I might get a little closer to

190

center stage in her affections. I was being broken to the marriage harness and, despite my basic loathings and thrashings, was beginning to enjoy it.

'Isn't that dangerous?' Angelina asked as we reached the ground and the double row of soldiers of the honor guard snapped to attention with a resounding crash and clatter. There must have been at least a thousand of them and each one was armed with a gaussrifle.

'Weapons have been incapacitated, that was part of the agreement.'

'But can we trust them?'

'Absolutely. One thing they know how to do is to take orders.'

We strolled on towards the reception buildings, between the rows of gaudy glittering soldiers, erect as statues with their rifles at present arms.

'I'll show you,' I said and led her over to the nearest soldier while the pram turned to follow us. He was tall, erect, big-jawed, steel-eyed, everything a soldier should be.

'Right shoulder-HARMS!' I barked in my best parade ground manner. He obeyed instantly with a great deal of snappy exactitude. Gray haired too, he must have been at the game for a long time.

'Inspection . . . wait for it . . . HARMS!'

He snapped the weapon down across his chest and with a double clack-clack opened the inspection port and extended the rifle. I seized it and looked inside the receiver. Spotless. I held it up to the sky and looked down the barrel and saw only unrelieved blackness.

'There's something blocking the barrel.'

'Yes, sir. Orders, sir.'

'What is it?'

'Lead, sir. Melted it and poured it in myself.'

'An excellent weapon. Carry on, trooper.' I hurled it

back at him and he caught and rattled it efficiently. There was something about him.

'Don't I know you, trooper?'

'Perhaps, sir, I've done duty on many planets. I was a colonel once.'

There was a distant glint in his eyes when he said this, but it quickly faded. Of course. I hadn't recognised him without his beard. He was the officer that Kraj had watching me, who had tried to shoot me when we first landed on Burada.

'I knew that man, high ranking officer,' I told Angelina as we strolled on.

'Very little chance for that kind of work now. He should be happy he has a job that keeps him out in the fresh air. It's amazing that they all seem to be taking it so well.'

'They have little choice. When their empire collapsed they flocked back here to Cliaand and found out that all their mineral and power resources had been exhausted during the invasion years and they had never noticed it. So it was either farm or go hungry. I understand that the agriculture is going just fine right now. And the gray men are gone. Inskipp sent agents in and found they had all packed up and left. To cause trouble elsewhere, I suppose. We are going to have to track them to their home planet one of these days.'

'Nasty people. That's where a globe-buster bomb would do some good.'

'Not in front of the children,' I said, patting her hand. 'You don't want them to get wrong thoughts about their mother.'

'They'll get some right ones. And I'm still suspicious of these ex-warrior types.'

'Don't be. We had political agents in here after the breakdown. Issuing orders, and orders are one thing they know how to take. All things considered they have been quite good about it.'

Angelina sniffed, still not convinced. 'I wonder what bright boy thought up the tourist routine – and suggested we come on the first tour ship?'

'I did. Guilty on both counts. And don't look daggers at me. They need something that will keep them busy and bring in foreign exchange and that sort of thing, and tourism is about all a planet without resources can manage. They have swimming and skiing and all the usual things, plus a deadly sort of fascination for the people they once invaded. It will work out, you just wait and see.'

Hordes of uniformed porters jostled for our baggage, then led the way with the bags to the surface transportation. Things had changed mightily since my first visit to this planet. They seemed to be enjoying themselves, too. I don't think they were ever cut out to be a warrior race and interstellar conquerors. For old times' sake I had registered us at the Zlato-Zlato where I had first stayed, still the most luxurious hotel in town. The doorman's manners were better this time and the desk clerk even bowed as we came up.

'Welcome to Cliaand, General and Mrs. James diGriz and sons. May your stay here be an enjoyable one.'

Traveling with a title always helps, even more so on this world. I looked around the lobby and then at the clerk.

'Ostrov! Is that you?' I said. He bowed again.

'I am Ostrov, indeed sir, but I am afraid you have the better of me.'

'Sorry. Couldn't expect you to recognize me with my own face, or a reasonable facsimile. The last time you talked to me you thought I was a creature named Kraj, and before that you knew me as Vaska Hulja.'

'Vaska – can it be you! It is, I do believe, the voice, of course.' Then his own voice sank. 'I hope you will accept my apology at this late date. I never did feel right about helping that Kraj to capture you. Even though I was unconscious for a day and a half, I was still rather happy you had escaped. I know you were a spy and all that, but...'

'Say no more. The matter is closed and I prefer to think of you as the roommate of our drinking days.'

'Most kind. Would you grant me the courtesy of shaking your hand?'

We shook and I looked at him curiously.

'You've changed, for the better I think. Put on a little weight, polished up the old manners.'

'Thank you, Vaska. Most kind. Stopped drinking so I have to watch my diet now. And I don't have to worry about flying those filthy spaceships any more. My family were always innkeepers, traditional trade and all that. Until the draft got me. A pleasure to return to something I know, and right at the top too as you can see. Shortage of good hotel men now. If you will sign here.'

He handed me the pen and continued in the same neutral voice, only not as loudly.

'I hope you will pardon my saying this is a bit of emergency, so please don't jump or turn around. But there has been a man staying here ever since we opened, one of Kraj's men I do believe, and he has the staff terrified. I didn't know what he wanted until this moment. I believe he is after you and I hope you are armed. He is coming from the right, behind you, wearing a plum jacket and yellow striped hat.'

It was a holiday – and I was unarmed. For the first time in a long time. I swore silently that it would be the last. Then I remembered Angelina and saw her bending over the robopram again.

'I don't wish to bother you, dearest,' I said, smiling, and

194

itchy feeling crawling up my back and into my skull. 'But the man in the plum jacket coming up behind me is an assassin. Do you think you could anything about it – and keep him alive if possible?'

'How sweet of you to ask!' she said, laughing, patting the pile of diapers in the pram.

I stepped back to the desk, watching her. Charming, relaxed, smiling, touching her hair.

Taking her time too. I opened my mouth to mention this fact – just as her arm snapped down. There was a muffled shriek behind me and I turned and ducked.

It was all over. Plum coat had lost his striped hat – and his pistol as well which was lying on the rug. He was reaching for the knife that projected from his upper arm, making little scrabbling motions. Then Angelina was at his side, chopping his neck and lowering his unconscious figure to the floor.

'Holiday world, indeed,' she sniffed, but I knew she was enjoying herself.

'You'll get a medal for this, my sweet. The Corps will take care of this lad and I imagine they will extract information about his home planet, which will be a relief.' I turned back to Ostrov.

'Thanks for saving my life.'

'Not at all, sir. I always believe that it is the little extra services that count. Now – may I show you to your room?'

'You may, and a drink as well. You'll join us in a glass, won't you?'

'Well, just this once, seeing as how it is a special occasion. And I must say that you are a lucky man to have a wife who shares your same enthusiasm and talents.'

'It was a match made in crime and some day I may tell you all about it.'

I looked on fondly while my Angelina neatly wiped her

knife on the unconscious man's shirt, then stowed it back among the diapers. I was sure that when the children got older they would appreciate her talents.

She was the sort of mother every boy should have.

From the living hell of her watery grave she rises again . . .

THE NIGHT BOAT

By Robert R. McCammon

Deep under the calm water of a Caribbean
lagoon, salvage diver David Moore discovers a
sunken Nazi U-boat entombed in the sand. A
mysterious relic from the last war. Slowly the U-
boat rises from the depths laden with a long-dead
crew, cancerous with rot, mummified for eternity.
Or so Moore thought.

**UNTIL HE HEARD THE DEEP,
HOLLOW BOOM OF SOMETHING
HAMMERING WITH FEVERISH
INTENSITY . . . SOMETHING
DESPERATELY TRYING TO GET OUT!**

If you've read either of Robert McCammon's
other horror masterpieces, you won't be disap-
pointed with **THE NIGHT BOAT**, but if this is
your first McCammon encounter, be prepared for
a bit of a shock!

HORROR   0 7221 5871 8   £1.25

Robert R. McCammon's
BAAL
and
BETHANY'S SIN
are also available in Sphere Books

WHAT TURNS MEN INTO MEAT-HUNGRY SAVAGES . . .?

FAMINE

by GRAHAM MASTERTON

When the grain crop failed in Kansas it seemed like an isolated incident and no one took too much notice. Except Ed Hardesty. Then the blight spread to California's fruit harvest – and from there, like wildfire, throughout the nation . . .

'The Greek-looking man said: 'This food in here – you think that you're going to keep it all to yourself? All of it? Just because you're a store-keeper you think you've got some God-given right to survive while everybody else starves?'

Nicolas didn't even want to think about it. He said: 'I'm giving you three. You understand me? Three, and then I shoot.'

The first shot missed. The revolver bucked in his hands, and he heard the bang of broken glass at the back of the store, followed by a sudden rush of green olives from three broken jars. He fired again before he could allow himself to think, and the Greek's shoulder burst apart in a spray of gory catsup. And then there was a deep, deafening *bavvooom*! and Nicolas realized with strange slow horror that the Greek had fired back at him with his shotgun, and that he'd been hit, badly hit, in the belly and the thighs . . .'

GENERAL FICTION   0 7221 6003 8   £1.75

JOE POYER

TUNNEL WAR

POLITICAL DYNAMITE!

In 1911 Europe was rushing headlong towards world war. And beneath the English Channel a massive tunnel was already under construction. When fire wreaked havoc in an unfinished tunnel shaft, James Bannerman, the project chief, smelt trouble. Further deadly 'accidents' confirmed his suspicions – the project was being systematically destroyed by a team of professional saboteurs.

Bannerman already faced an impossible choice: sacrifice the tunnel – or the lives of his men. But nothing had quite prepared him for the devastating web of murder and conspiracy that stretched from Ireland to Germany to the heart of Britain's political arena and which threatened to destroy everything he'd ever fought for – including his life . . .

ADVENTURE THRILLER   0 7221 7027 0   £1.50
And, don't miss Joe Poyer's other thrilling novels, also available in Sphere Books:

**For twenty-five years it grew
in the shadows—tonight it waits for
Amy in . . .**

THE FUNHOUSE

CARNIVAL OF TERROR

A novel by
Owen West
based on a screenplay by
Larry Block

Tonight Amy and her friends are spending the
night at the carnival. And whilst they enjoy all
the fun of the fair they will visit the funhouse, a
place for gondola rides, gory delights and
midnight terror.
But there is unspeakable Evil waiting for Amy in
the dark labyrinths of the funhouse, a secret
Evil that began twenty-five years ago, when a
lonely woman destroyed her monstrous
offspring, and a violently disturbed man vowed
to exact his terrible revenge.
Now it's Amy's turn to keep her date with horror
as she enters the funhouse – for
A CARNIVAL OF TERROR!

HORROR   0 7221 9001 8   £1.25

WILL

The remarkable autobiography of

G. GORDON LIDDY

WHAT MADE LIDDY KEEP SILENCE WHEN HIS
FELLOW WATERGATE CONSPIRATORS WERE
PREPARED TO TALK? WHAT MADE LIDDY
PREPARED TO KILL E. HOWARD HUNT AND
NEWSPAPER COLUMNIST JACK ANDERSON?
WHAT MADE LIDDY OFFER TO BE
ASSASSINATED? WHAT MAKES HIM SUCH AN
EXTRAORDINARY MAN?
    READ *WILL* AND YOU'LL FIND OUT . . .

G. Gordon Liddy's refusal to talk about his role
in Watergate resulted in a prison sentence of
twenty years. After serving nearly five years,
President Carter reduced Liddy's sentence. Now
Liddy is a free man. And now he is prepared to
reveal the truth.

'What is most striking about WILL is what it
reveals about the kind of man who will do
anything to stop those he sees as his country's
enemies' *Time*

AUTOBIOGRAPHY   0 7221 5550 6   £1.75

Heart of War

by John Masters

January 1 1916: Europe is bleeding to death as the corpses rot from Poland to Gallipoli in the cruel grip of the Great War ...

HEART OF WAR

– follows the fate and fortunes of the Rowland family and those people bound up in their lives, the Cate squirearchy, the Strattons who manage the Rowland-owned factory, and the humble, multi-talented Gorse family.

HEART OF WAR

– during the years 1916 and 1917, the appalling slaughter of the Somme and Passchendaele cuts deep into the hearts of the British people as military conscription looms over Britain for the first time in a thousand years.

HEART OF WAR

– is the second self-contained volume in a trilogy entitled LOSS OF EDEN. It is probably the crowning achievement in the long and distinguished career of one of our leading contemporary novelists.

GENERAL FICTION   0 7221 0467 7   **£1.95**

And, also by John Masters in Sphere Books:
NOW, GOD BE THANKED
NIGHTRUNNERS OF BENGAL
THE FIELD-MARSHAL'S MEMOIRS
FANDANGO ROCK
THE HIMALAYAN CONCERTO

A SELECTION OF BESTSELLERS FROM **SPHERE**

FICTION

I, SAID THE SPY	Derek Lambert	£1.75	☐
HEART OF WAR	John Masters	£1.95	☐
REVELATIONS	Phyllis Naylor	£1.50	☐
LOVING	Danielle Steel	£1.50	☐

FILM & TV TIE-INS

MUPPET MANNERS	Pat Relf	95p	☐
FOZZIE'S BIG BOOK OF SIDE-SPLITTING JOKES	Pat Relf	95p	☐
THE PROFESSIONALS SERIES	Ken Blake	£1.00 each	☐

NON-FICTION

A WAY TO DIE	Rosemary & Victor Zorza	£1.50	☐
MARY	Patricia Collins	£1.50	☐
THE CLASSIFIED MAN	Susanna M. Hoffman	£1.50	☐
WILL	G. Gordon Liddy	£1.75	☐
ROGET'S THESAURUS		£2.10	☐

All Sphere Books are available at your local bookshop or newsagent, or can be ordered direct from the publisher. Just tick the titles you want and fill in the form below.

Name ───────────────────────────

Address ─────────────────────────

─────────────────────────────────

Write to Sphere Books, Cash Sales Department, P.O. Box 11, Falmouth, Cornwall TR10 9EN.

Please enclose a cheque or postal order to the value of the cover price:

UK: 40p for the first book, 18p for the second book and 13p for each additional book ordered to a maximum charge of £1.49.

OVERSEAS: 60p for the first book plus 18p per copy for each additional book.

BFPO & EIRE: 40p for the first book, 18p for the second book plus 13p per copy for the next 7 books; thereafter 7p per book.

Sphere Books reserve the right to show new retail prices on covers which may differ from those previously advertised in the text or elsewhere, and to increase postal rates in accordance with the PO.